Statue of
Limitations

Also by Jon Konrath

Fiction:

Decision Paralysis (2024)

The Failure Cascade (2020)

Ranch: The Musical (2019)

Book of Dreams (2018)

Help Me Find My Car Keys and We Can Drive Out! (2017)

Vol. 13 (2016)

He (2015)

The Memory Hunter (2014)

Atmospheres (2014)

Thunderbird (2013)

Sleep Has No Master (2012)

The Earworm Inception (2012)

Fistful of Pizza (2011)

Rumored to Exist (2002)

Summer Rain (2000)

Nonfiction:

The Necrokonicon (2006)

Dealer Wins (2004)

Tell Me a Story About the Devil (2003)

Statue of Limitations

Jon Konrath

Rumored Books
Oakland, CA
Rumored.com

ISBN: 978-1-942086-23-9

RB-1

Dedication 1

Dream Report 10/18/24 3

The moist adiabatic lapse rate varies from 1.1 °C to 2.8 °C (2 °F to 5 °F) per 1,000 feet 9

Pin Six for Satan...13

The Flavor of Noise 19

Simple Man 23

When the protocol activates... mercy is deleted! 29

20190911 33

No Zodiacs or Almanacs..37

The Gamut of Human Disaster, Now Available at Sears...39

Live Fast, Eat Limestone..43

Dumb story ideas that didn't make it 49

I AM CHARLES FOSTER KANE, AND I'M GONNA GET MEDIEVAL ON YOUR ASS! 53

The Silver and Gold Manalishi (With the Two Prong Crown) 61

Terms and Conditions 65

#ColchicineLifestyle 71

When Dream and Dumb Unite 77

Surge Country...87

Orem Chipotle 91

A bad rower blames the oar 95

What We Talk About When We Talk About Sodium Hypochlorite 99

Situs inversus is not a black metal band...103

PI IS TWO, GOD DAMN IT 111

An unrelated story about shitty pancakes and nuclear war.......................................117

From the 2023 Breyerlin Baseline Cognitive Performance Survey (BBCPS) 127

Intestinal Vestibule 131

Corporate Sanitation of Cadaveric Beef Through Mechanical Violence......................135

Head Like a Hole...139

Skippy: Unfinity...147

Infinite McDonald's..151

Statue of Limitations...155

About the Author...161

Dedication

This book is dedicated to the city planner from Anchorage who bought me one of every item on the Taco Bell Express menu during a snowstorm in Dallas, Texas in 1993 and told me the story about how his brother was in a medically-induced coma because he tried using a belt sander for self-surgery and accidentally split the two halves of his brain, which increased his United States Chess Federation Elo ranking by 400 points.

Dream Report 10/18/24

I'm wandering Bloomington, or a bizarro version of it. Staying in an alternate reality version of the Mitchell Street house where I lived in 1991-1993, a tiny closet of a room in a 27-bedroom, 3-bathroom house. The campus has significantly doubled or tripled in density, scores of tall brutalist tower buildings that look like they're from the Soviet Union circa 1963. They've installed a large four-reactor nuclear power plant in the middle of the arboretum, and looking at all the poured concrete involved, I know it's only a matter of time before the entire lower half of the state is radioactive.

I'm in the early stages with a girl I met from Google Street View, who's both interested and uninterested in me. We haven't had sex but she's naked in my bed, talking about her high school's rugby team, who all went missing on a plane trip. I don't want to make the obvious cannibalism reference and ruin everything. And I'm fairly certain if I mention the movie or book *Alive* about the Uruguayan rugby team, she'll think I was talking about the Pearl Jam song. I am at that point where I am drunk with infatuation and want to spend every hour of the day with her. I need more, but I am suffocating because I know I can't get more. It's basically the same deal as the built-by-the-lowest-bidder-in-

Indiana nuclear power plant that we all know will catastrophically explode in the near future.

Later, in the bathroom, standing in front of a 1950s vanity mirror with a flickering fluorescent light overhead, trying to cut my hair with an old pair of Oster pet clippers. I have the same male pattern baldness as I do now, but the remaining hair is thick, black. I'm not sure if I'm supposed to shave it all off or keep some in the back to hide the oblong shape of my skull. I somehow mess up trimming it and accidentally shave a large patch of my temple bald and it looks like a radiation burn.

Walking or driving around campus... maybe I'm doing a bit of both. I keep thinking, "I know exactly where I'm going, I know the bones of this place" but I do not recognize a single landmark. The western part of campus now looked like Spain in some way, with Gaudi-like surreal architecture on the tall buildings and a Mercadillo sprawl of Barcelona's open-air markets. I'm amazed by all the small shops and bars in every alley and pocket of the city, because I remember a half-vacant town with nothing but the same generic pizza places and t-shirt stores. I wish I could find something from my past, but there's absolutely nothing there, only shops catering to people a generation younger than me.

I'm driving on what used to be State Road 446 or whatever it is called, the two-lane going out to Brown County. The numbers have been removed from every road in Indiana because math is woke. The roads are extremely winding, much more so than in reality, almost resembling a tightly-designed roller coaster. I'm on a downhill switchback, and in the distance someone has built a bunch of full-size Star Wars AT-AT walkers. As I get closer, in the middle of the road there are packs of elephants and rhinos blocking traffic, randomly colliding with cars. The highway turns into pure mud and everyone is sliding uncontrollably, running into large animals or other cars. My rental car, some little shitbox Hyundai or Kia, becomes impossible to drive, and the dashboard is full of red warning lights. I pull off the highway onto a gravel access road, and see the whole area is a movie backlot of some sort, with large hangers full of disassembled sets and lighting equipment.

After the car cools off and dries a bit, I drive back to the mall to find an AutoZone or similar and use their scan gauge to reset the warning lights. The only place that resembles a car shop has been turned into a warehouse store that has the branding of an old Kinney shoes but they sell bowls made out of human skulls. I go inside the main mall and it's now a bizarro version of College Mall, with a completely different look and layout done to look like an EPCOT Center version of the 1996 Olympics bombing. They built a brand new Sears to replace the one that was torn down in 2015 and replaced with a grocery store, but the new one is already abandoned, maybe even before it opened.

I can't piece together where the old mall stores were in the Nineties. Nothing lines up with the current reality, making me wonder if the entire mall was demolished at some point and rebuilt as a 2010s monstrosity of generic Simon post-mall architecture, or if I'm trapped in a five-dimensional tesseract like the movie *Interstellar*. I get excited about the prospect that I can possibly communicate with my past self by influencing gravity and maybe pushing books off shelves in a morse code pattern. I try to visualize the strings that represent the aspect of fourth-dimensional time in this world as a physical aspect, but then remember that the Nineties me doesn't know morse code and this won't work. I could possibly encapsulate TCP/IP packets in a serial format if I moved around objects in the correct patterns, but I can't remember if Serial Line Internet Protocol or Point-to-Point Protocol was the preferred format in 1992. Also there are no longer any book stores and even IU's official "book" store in the student union no longer sells books.

There's an anchor store that looks boarded up, but when I get closer, it's open for business and bustling with customers. It's called Schlomo's Deli, Grocery, and Alcoholics Social Concern. It's an old-time halal butcher and grocer, but they have meetings for an alternative version of AA in the same area where they sell corned beef sandwiches on picnic tables. All the workers look like stereotypical old Jewish butchers from New York sent in from central casting. I am not an alcoholic but think maybe I need to find something, get into a recovery program to stop my horrible nostalgia problem, attachment anxiety, and lack of purpose in life. I pick up their free pamphlet called *The Book* without anyone approaching me, and I promise myself to read it later.

I want to go find my car and leave, but every exit to the mall goes through a Victoria's Secret, and I don't want to walk through Victoria's Secret. I eventually find a fire exit that leads to a futuristic concrete tunnel that looks like the one in *Logan's Run*. I walk in it for about four days and emerge in Carhenge, Nebraska. Rick Wakeman runs up to me and says he just invented MIDI keyboards and he needs $10,000 in Apple gift cards to buy a new hooded sweatshirt with a cape on the back. I tell him to point me to a curry shop and he doesn't get the joke and ignores me.

I wake up and for a few minutes while I'm still half-asleep, I feel an overwhelming need to read *The Book* and fix my life. I try to google it, but then realize I'm an idiot.

The moist adiabatic lapse rate varies from 1.1 °C to 2.8 °C (2 °F to 5 °F) per 1,000 feet

47 auto fatalities per second are caused by teenagers abusing insulin. It's the latest craze, bored high school dropouts trying to cop a buzz by shooting Novolin while driving at high speed and masturbating, then slipping into a hypoglycemic coma and crashing into oncoming traffic. I think this started on TikTok, I don't know. Someone said this is how James Dean died, but I've tried jerking off in a Porsche 550, and unless he got some ribs removed or was three feet tall, it's almost impossible. And he died 27 years before Eli Lilly started selling Humulin, but it's possible he was a time traveler. I also don't know his exact height.

Someone's screaming "I'M A VEGAN" back in coach class, and the pilot just came on the intercom and said he's about to blow all of the emergency exits if the woman doesn't shut the fuck up. I'm looking around trying to find the undercover air marshal with the ankle holster gun, but maybe they don't do that anymore. A flight attendant could force-feed the dude a ham sandwich for sedation purposes, but they barely have food on planes these days. They forced all 167 of us to split a single 10-ounce bag of mini pretzels. No alcohol, of course. And the in-flight movie was *Glitter* dubbed in Arabic.

"Curse of the cumulonimbus. Windows shattered for miles. Every skylight, pure destruction. Shitter's full!" She looked like Randy Quaid after he completely hit bottom, with a little Tonya Harding blank stare mixed in for effect. She yelled at people because her bank sent her a chip card and she said she was on a diet. She'd later fly to North Korea with her church group and end up in a prison camp, eventually slipping into a ten-year coma for trying to eat a piece of a potato out of a field latrine. They sent that little kid with the glasses from *Jerry Maguire* to negotiate her release, but he got detained at the Beijing airport by a group of tourists who wanted to scream "SHOW ME A MONEY" at him for twelve hours straight. She eventually died of sepsis and anal bleeding, long after she was out of the news cycle. The kid fell in love with China and moved there, though. I think they have free health care, or at least it's cheaper than what you get on the SAG child actor plan.

Most midair collisions happen on clear days. It's pitch black outside with a tropical storm hitting the coast of Jamaica at 240 miles per hour, so I'm not worried. I wrote an inspirational letter to Friedrich Weyerhäuser, the timber baron of the Pacific Northwest, by carving hieroglyphics into my left arm with a #11 X-Acto knife. I told him about how they started injecting cheese into hot dogs and that the band

Cattle Decapitation played the Sängerhalle Saulheim concert hall he sponsored in Germany in 1904. A pilot can expect a wind shear zone in a temperature inversion whenever the windspeed at 2,000 to 4,000 feet above the surface is at least 25 knots. I never liked Mondays.

Pin Six for Satan

The death metal bowling attendant carefully arranged a dozen low-grade cafeteria pizzas in a pentagram on lane four of the no-longer-an-official-AMF-center bowling alley. His black metal corpse paint ran with sweat, and each time he fidgeted with the long strands of comb-over hair that unconvincingly tried to cover his bald pate, they became stained with white greasepaint. "PIN SIX FOR SATAN!" he screamed to nobody. "PIN SIX FOR SATAN!" He squinted, tried to read the animated scoreboard displays on the far wall, but couldn't. He needed glasses, was having trouble seeing the road when he drove at like a hundred in the wrong lane, but drug store cheaters wouldn't cut it for distance, and he didn't have the insurance to hit the optical place in the mall or the cash to go to an online one. LASIK was the dream. Tiger Woods had it done, and he depends on his eyesight to make millions. Or at least he did, before he became a go-to joke for hack comedians. Maybe they do this in Mexico now.

The kiddie birthday bowling party on lane five demanded a full refund because of the Satanist's antics, an endless stream of "can I speak to your manager" helicopter parent brutality directed at the hourly workers who didn't give a shit. One of the moms claimed her child was allergic to indefinite articles, and the "take a penny/leave a penny" tray was going to cause her precious angel to go into anaphylactic shock. She epi-penned the kid five times for no reason, and the tot's pulse was at like 400 when the paramedics showed up. The party still managed to roll ten rounds of bumpers-up kiddie-ball and eat fifty thousand calories of grease and fat before calling 911. The owner of the establishment eventually woke up from his deep hibernation in the back office and used a five-iron to beat the shit out of the Satanist wannabe for screwing up the lane wood. It took the Guatemalan janitor six hours to get all of the tomato sauce stains out of the teak boards using a steam machine on low and an enzymatic wood bleach.

"You can have a seizure from a black light. It's not just strobes," she said. "It's any light, especially if the bulbs aren't organic." He did not believe her, at least about the seizure thing. He knew about using black lights to detect bodily fluids, because he spent a lot of time jerking off in motels. He had a flashback to a La Quinta in the Mexican part of Denver, a hotel so old, they still used physical keys for the doors, even in the 2000s. He ordered one of everything from the Taco Bob next door, and after settling in for a night of endless carbs and porn, found the motor lodge had a wide-open Wi-Fi connection, no passwords, nothing: just a full-on fat pipe to the internet. He immediately started mirroring ten different nudie sites to his hard drive at the same time, scraping the open directories *en masse* with esoteric wget commands, grabbing thousands of jpegs and mpegs of barely legal amateurs and bored housewives and all-anal casting sessions. Because why not — abuse every free wireless connection while you can. You never know when you'll be stuck in an airport for days with only that high-price wireless that never works anyway and charges you by the byte.

* * *

A school bus thief amassed a motley collection of at least a dozen Blue Bird buses. He primarily stole the Blue Bird All American buses with the Cummins VT555 V8 diesel front-engine configuration, circa 1975-1985. Nobody knew why he was fixated on Type-D transit vehicles. Maybe he had a family member killed by someone trying to pass a stopped bus. Maybe he wanted to convert them into hippie campers running on french fry oil. Maybe he was a big fan of that Plasmatics video for "The Damned" where punk rocker Wendy O. Williams drove a school bus through a wall of TVs and blew it up. (That was one of the *Beavis and Butthead* video-watching segments where Beavis went nuts about fire, and it was subsequently cut out of future airings when some stupid redneck kid who didn't even have cable TV burned down his family's single-wide trailer.) Or it's possible he had a commercial Class A license with a school bus endorsement and was trying to get his moneys' worth.

The police never found him. They did dig up a mass grave they stumbled upon in their search, but it was unrelated. Some old cult that worshipped Slim-Fast shakes and had an ultra-charismatic leader who allegedly lost 500 pounds drinking pond water and protein supplements. They wanted to DNA test the corpses, but this was a local sheriff's department, and they spent all of their budget for the next five years on a crate of AR-15 rifles, the actual capitol-C Colt law enforcement version that costs like twice as much as a generic AR-15 you can buy at every flea market across America. Maybe some federal cold-case project would figure it out twenty years from now. Probably not.

The sheriff announced they would do a press conference at the Motel 3 out by the toll road, but they couldn't book the lobby because a swinger's convention was in town, and gave all the housekeeping staff hepatitis. No word on what kind, but it sounded like A and C were both going around. They ended up playing a slideshow on the local news, just a bunch of text generated on a Commodore 64 the station used for the last thirty years for weather reports and community announcements. It was an all-caps wall of light blue on blue letters. The phones rang off the hook at the news desk because old people didn't want to read, they wanted *Wheel of Fortune*, god damn it.

Within a year, that Sheriff got hooked on PCP and ended up dead. Sure, angel dust is technically not addictive like crack or heroin, but anything can become a bad habit if you fuck up enough. He got off on snorting a few lines of the pure Parke-Davis veterinarian shit they had in the seizure room, then driving a squad car at top speed on the city streets, trying to hit the 137 MPH governor on the cop-issue

Crown Vic. Sure it's fun, but it doesn't make for a sustainable hobby. He almost hit 137 once, but forgot that Florence Avenue bottoms out into a cul-de-sac in the 2500 block, and drove straight through a tri-level, killing himself and nine other people. Took out their holiday decorations and nativity set too, so the War on Christmas crowd went nuts, started stockpiling ammunition again. (When don't they?)

The Flavor of Noise

An Army vet with PTSD hung out at the McDonald's in the mall food court, asking people for extra nugget sauce packs, which he used to brew wine in the toilets in the bathroom. (Ketchup works too, but there's much more flavor and body if you use sweet and sour sauce.) He was deployed in Afghanistan five times, but was a 42R, an Army musician, and played tuba in a quartet that hung out in the baggage area of the Kandahar International Airport. They performed jazz standards to incoming passengers, twelve hours a day, six days a week: "Autumn Leaves," "Blue Monk," "Take the A Train," and occasionally "My Favorite Things" around Christmas. The closest thing he had to a traumatic experience was losing his valve oil at the Frankfurt airport. Some people gave him sauce packets or a dollar. The McDonald's workers ignored him. As long as he didn't start screaming about McMurder or Jesus, he wasn't on their radar.

Jesus the mall walker saw him every day as he completed his eight loops, a quarter-mile per loop. He listened to an FM radio that looked like the big earphones luggage handlers wear on the tarmac, except with a long whip antenna mounted to one earpiece. His name was Jesus. Not to be confused with a Jesus mall walker, handing out little comic books about the evils of Catholicism and shaming the kids at Hot Topic for their unnatural hair colors. After his two miles, he strutted back and forth on a bed of hot coals the shopping center kept burning as a service to their customers who were Tony Robbins fans. (Most people used them to light cigarettes.)

Twenty-three female high school volleyball players swarmed the IT'SUGAR candy store, looking for mass calories, even though the doping compounds they were abusing were probably causing hyperglycemia. The shortest of the group was six-foot-eight. The tallest one looked to be at least eight feet and change. A doctor in the coffee shop watched the procession of teen athletes and theorized something in the groundwater near their town caused a pituitary gland hyperactivity. If they could bottle it, a fortune could be made selling it to amateur athletes and travel sport parents.

The doctor went back to furiously brain-dumping his latest idea. He wanted to patent a combination EpiPen and Narcan injector, for people who overdose on heroin that contains trace amounts of peanut products. He took notes in a tiny notebook bound in human flesh, scribbling on the pages with a stubby golf pencil he found in the church confession box. He never got the patent, but he was briefly famous for his extensive collection of Japanese dental pornography.

Jon Konrath

Simple Man

At the post office, a Ronnie Van Zant-looking dude in a Skoal t-shirt from 1974 in front of me kept humming the song "Tequila" and eyeing me as I fastened stamp after stamp to the package I had to mail overseas. The impossible-to-use web page said it took 247 of the 23-cent stamps to mail a one-ounce letter to Tokyo, ground rate, which would arrive six months later, if it even arrived at all. It was initially only 240 stamps, but the rate actually went up in the time it took me to pay for the postage at the counter. And this was a ten-pound box, so multiply that by 160. My brother moved to Occupied Japan to work in the cartoon industry, and couldn't find a place that sold dish drainers. Not sure if this was an ideological issue with their new leader, or maybe they culturally didn't like to leave dishes out to dry? I assembled him a care package of housewares and pornography, although I expected the whole thing to get seized or lost at sea.

I tried to block out the man's humming with a random chaotic album playing in my earbuds, but his humming was a specific tone or timbre that somehow got past the noise-cancellation algorithm. Maybe I could upgrade to the next-generation headphones with New and Improved noise cancellation or buy a new phone that could play stuff at 250 decibels, enough to turn my skull into a thick paste. I'd pay extra for that feature. I'd even pay a bullshit monthly subscription for it.

I hated the main post office. I mean, I hate all post offices, but this particular one unnerved me. The grand Valhalla of a building looked like a make-work government project built at the end of the groovy Sixties: all poured concrete, with high ceilings, wood trim everywhere, and a burnt sienna carpet that had been cleaned once in 1986, and now smelled like the kennel at a humane society. Fifty thousand square feet of real estate, and they had exactly one service window open, with a clerk too busy doing the word jumble to even acknowledge the existence of customers. The trip to the Post Office, the long wait in line and then me giving up took twenty minutes. Also, they were only open from ten to three, with a two-hour lunch.

One interesting thing about the location was a plaque in the dirt lawn out front that described how an armed postal inspector once killed an anarchist who knew the guy that knew the guy who shot President Garfield. I guess the anarchist got in an argument with a postal teller about turning in some International Reply Coupons, which the Post Office never wants to deal with, even though they are required by international law to honor them. (An International Reply Coupon, or IRC, is a small slip of paper with various official-looking seals or stamps on it. Any participating country's post office is required to exchange them for the amount of a postage stamp used to mail a letter internationally. They're

used because you can't mail a self-addressed stamped enve-
lope to someone in another country because you won't have
that country's stamps. It's a great idea, but nobody even
knows what they are anymore, and USPS employees hate
them, because are they supposed to give you the amount you
paid for it ten years ago, or the amount that postage is now?
This was actually exploited by Charles Ponzi, who realized
you could make money by buying cheap IRCs in one country and selling them in another, but dealing with slips of paper and pissed-off postal clerks doesn't scale, and the only
lasting legacy of this is that any get-rich-quick scheme is
named after Ponzi. Also, I have a fat stack of these IRCs
from my zine days, and no idea what to do with them.)
Things escalated with the guard, and he drew and fired. He
didn't know about the anarchist connection until the police
identified the body from dental records. It didn't say all of
this on the plaque — I had to look it up on Wikipedia, but
they say he was a socialist who performed mandatory abor-
tions, and that this would never happen if everyone was required to carry a full-auto rifle at all times in government
buildings.

I gave up on affixing rows and columns of stamps, and
wrapped the coil of postage around the letter like a ban-
dolier, or maybe the knot of a hangman's noose, which I
wished I had at that moment. (The hangman's knot, by the
way, is also called a Jack Ketch knot, named after the famous
British executioner of the 19th century. And I always tried to
tie my hangman's knots with thirteen coils, which I think

was in a Motörhead song, but it's almost impossible for me to make one with more than six or eight coils unless I grease the rope.) The stamps were self-adhesive, and stuck to my fingers like I was trying to unfold a cheese danish, the möbius strip of postage twisting everywhere. Far beyond the point of even remembering what I was mailing or why, I just wanted to get out of there in one piece and forget the entire afternoon.

A podcast now droned on in my headphones. I had one earbud in, one out, and reaffixed the loose plug to block my hearing. The transmission was a spoken-word experimental jazz bit where a trance DJ from Wales sampled all of Jack Kervorkian's speeches and cut-pasted the words so he was reading the Heaven's Gate cult's suicide notes, with David Koresh's heavy metal blues jam guitar looping in the background. It was like the triple crown of Nineties snuff suicide rock and roll revolution. Had a good beat, too. You just had to fast-forward through the twenty minutes of Audible and SquareSpace ads at the beginning.

Package mailed, allegedly. Who knows if it would make it. I was sure it wouldn't, and my brother would start some passive-aggressive shit in a family group chat I'm not in, blaming the perils of international shipping on me personally. Any attempt at doing someone a favor usually devolved into a "you can't win" scenario. I feel like my entire life is a series of expectations of me I can never meet. I'm hemorrhaging money to do favors nobody will acknowledge, or maybe I'll get a passive-aggressive complaint. The best investment I could make in myself is a high-yield nuclear warhead to start the apocalypse, but that damned SALT II treaty strikes again. And I don't know how many stamps it takes to mail the MIRV warheads off an RT-23 ICBM from Kazakhstan to the US.

I went to the remains of a strip mall next to the PO and watched a construction team tear down a junior high school amphitheater that was used as a bootleg church for the last few years after they banned schools in the county. I saw it on the news; they had a ceiling collapse that released a cloud of toxins so brutal even this flat-earth state government felt a duty to intervene. They soaked the structure with fire hoses pumping a mixture of Coca-Cola and kerosene to keep down the billowing asbestos dust so they could tear down the walls without killing everyone in the entire county. No masks, of course. These were Real Men, or at least they would be until they died of mesothelioma before they were 35.

I thought of a time I used to fuck out a cashier at a Long John Silver's in a similar shopping center, and she would give me free fountain soda as long as I brought my own cup. Her LJS was next to a True-Value hardware store where all the serial killers in town used to work, when they weren't busy abducting prostitutes and kidnapping victims. Free power tool rentals go a long way when you have to dismember corpses in your basement. You can make fast work of digging shallow graves when you can rent a Ditch Witch for free. Also they had a good coffee bar in the front of the hardware store, although I personally don't drink the stuff. I stuck with warm fountain soda from the LJS in a mop bucket, and tried to get autographs of the cashiers in case one of the killers made it big.

There was no way Coca-Cola slurry would stop this asbestos from killing me, I thought. I should wrap a piss-soaked bandana over my mouth, as a futile attempt at filtration. While digging through my backpack to find the handkerchief, I found the package I thought I just mailed, and would still need to buy another forty or fifty dollars of stamps to cover the rate change that occurred in the last five minutes. I also didn't need to take a piss because I was off liquids that week, so the handkerchief thing wasn't going to work anyway. You really can't win.

When the protocol activates... mercy is deleted!

Fatal Vengeance Protocol: Shadow of the Executioner is a direct-to-video action-adventure movie starring Steven Seagal, Brett Favre, and Rip Taylor. The tag line on the teaser poster was "They broke the rules. He broke their bones." It was filmed in 2012 and never released. 19 extras and stunt doubles were killed in a crash of a Chinese Chengdu J-20 stealth fighter. The air superiority aircraft did product placement for the Spangler Candy Company, dropping Bit-O-Honey chews onto a massive dance scene, then plowed into the ground at mach two. None of the film's billed cast was in the scene, but the high cost of the downed fifth-generation stealth fighter and the wrongful death lawsuits cost orders of magnitude more than the $100,000 budget for the picture. The insurance company shelved the project, put all shot footage and an editor's workprint in an underground vault that will be sealed until the year 2437, and attempted to scrub the web of any evidence that the project ever existed.

* * *

In March, Taco Bell announced they were reducing their menu to two items: plain tacos and Mountain Dew Baja Blast. Everything else would be retired and removed, and they planned a large funeral service where burritos, quesadillas, Mexican pizzas, chalupas, Crunchwrap Supremes, and gorditas would be thrown in a mass grave and covered with lava sauce and concrete. In the next 24 hours, over 17,000 Taco Bell employees were killed or wounded in outbreaks of violence across the world. The Taco Bell corporation countered by announcing a global "We Fucked Up!" ad campaign and a new menu with 6,247 items on it, including hamburgers, taco burgers, pizza tacos, taco pizzas, hamburger taco pizzas, and at least 167 different variations on nachos, including breakfast nachos, dessert nachos, sport nachos, and a tater tot bacon pizza M&M meatloaf waffle fried chicken ice cream taco nachos.

They also introduced their new euthanasia nachos, which contained high doses of morphine, diazepam, and propranolol, and was only available in the seven states that currently supported euthanasia laws. The ads used an animated cartoon Jack Kevorkian, reminiscent of the animated dancing old guy in the Six Flags commercials, who looked like Uncle Junior from *The Sopranos* on methamphetamine.

* * *

Two people beat the shit out of each other in the dining room of a Wendy's over the unavailability of Szechuan sauce for their off-brand chicken McNuggets. I can't tell which one works there and which one is the customer. I guess Wendy's doesn't pay for uniforms anymore, or maybe the cashiers are crowd-sourced through an app or something. And I don't want to tell them about the fact that Szechuan sauce was only available at McDonald's briefly in 1998 to promote the movie *Mulan*. Getting drawn into this fight is a major loss-loss. Also, I found 47 cents of loose change inside my spicy chicken sandwich. Three dimes, three nickels, and two pennies. You'd think a quarter, two dimes, and two pennies would have greater odds of going unnoticed, weight-wise. That's only 15.206 grams versus 26.804 grams. Four dimes, a nickel, and two pennies sounds lighter, based on a dime being smaller, but that's 19.072 grams. Don't get me started on how Wendy's had a 1/3 pounder burger and nobody bought it because they thought a quarter-pounder weighed more. I'm going to die on an operating table while three surgeons in their twenties look up how to do an endovascular repair of an aortic aneurysm on YouTube.

* * *

Someone told her the President was making meat illegal, so she made big plans, bought a suicide bomber vest at Wal-Mart. Explosives not included, so what's the use, you can't get C-4 over the counter anymore, and that fertilizer and motor oil bit isn't going to work. This aggression will not stand! I think she got arrested by a postal inspector and became a famous born-again once she got in the pen. Everyone who's forced to watch black-and-white TV and brew their own wine in the toilet loves Jesus. Super-high Q numbers with that demo.

Statue of Limitations

* * *

Mick Mars got on a health kick during retirement and started eating salads so much, he tried to market a Mötley Crüe-ton. One of the five flavors was Wild Side Ranch. Nobody bought them, because some artificial ingredient in the recipe gave everyone uncontrollable diarrhea, even if they didn't eat them and were just within ten feet of an open bag. He almost managed to sell the company to Unilever, but BMG Rights Management blocked the sale. 100 years later, scientists found out the product was a perfect agent to chelate toxins like mercury or lead from body fat.

20190911

I'm on the roof of the parking garage eating a jumbo bag of vintage Brach's bridge mix I had to buy in China because the Brach's corporation stopped making it and the store brands are all garbage. I threw out the caramels (dental trauma) and shoveled everything else in my fat mouth as fast as possible before the chocolate melted. My cell phone is wavering between zero and one bars, and none of my memes will load. I've been thinking about checking into a hotel and using their WiFi, sleeping in the bed for hours and binge-watching cable TV. It's a solid plan, except the Hyatt House next to the mall is $425 a night, and their WiFi is garbage. I keep eating — I want to make it to the bottom of the bag before all the pieces turn into soup, and fuck soup. I should have worn plastic gloves.

My apartment was off-limits until the next day at noon. The super was pumping the basement full of sarin gas to get rid of a bug infestation. I think sarin is illegal, but lots of things are illegal. This is what I get for renting a place from a guy in the Aum Shinrikyo Japanese doomsday cult. I felt almost offended that none of the members showed up to push their agenda on me, give me the spiel and ask for a credit card or ACH banking transfer information. The rent wasn't even that cheap, which is the first thing everyone asks me when I say I rent from a cult. All the appliances were top-notch, though. And no bugs, or at least there wouldn't be after tomorrow.

Spent two hours yesterday afternoon trying to research if Big Bird from *Sesame Street* was an apex predator and hunted humans. Most references in the show have him chomping on birdseed or things made from seeds, like a birdseed pizza. Apex predators, at least in the bird family, are usually carnivores. (Vultures eat carrion; owls eat rodents; eagles eat fish.) The average omnivore bird eats about half their weight per day, and Big Bird's probably weighing in at about 300 pounds. I don't even know how you would get 150 pounds of seeds per day in Manhattan. Also Big Bird's eye placement on the front of his face suggests he has precision binocular vision with high depth perception, a feature that's only prominent in predators who hunt. Don't fall down this rabbit hole.

I must have dozed off in the car with the engine running and the AC blasting at like 47 degrees. I bought a new chip for the Toyota so I could set the temperature down to zero Kelvin. It used to go down to 65, then to LO and no further settings beyond that. It works great but you have to press the down arrow 525 times to get to the bottom range of temperature.

Had a weird dream about a colony of sheep-fuckers who started a homeopathic bookstore with magazines and paperbacks you could eat. They were supposed to cure cancer, which is always a tip-off that they won't. Gluten-free, of course. And no GMOs. The company spokesman was a beady-eyed wooly mammal enthusiast who ran constant YouTube ads about how eating meat dictionaries three to five times a week would completely stop any carcinoma in its tracks. "I don't care if the doctors already lopped off your arms and legs. We can grow 'em back. Guaranteed!" (He air-quoted the word "guaranteed.") "Click the link below! Payment plans available! God bless! Fake meat is murder!"

The total cold gave me insane dreams about being back in New York, where every building was turned into a Duane Reade drug store and they banned walking to boost Uber profits. I went to the Duane Reade on the corner of Ave B and 2nd to see The GG Allin Parsons Project play a set. They got halfway through "Eye in the Sky (You Fucking Whore)" and the cops showed up in riot turnout gear with teargas. I stole a jug of clear protein supplement and escaped before they started firing rubber bullets into the crowd. A few blocks later, I found a hot dog vendor who wasn't paying attention and dumped a pound of the synthetic protein powder in his hot dog water, accidentally inventing the latest health food craze for the high protein lifestyle: protein hot dog jello cubes. No patent, no royalties. Typical. Woke up and thought the whole thing was real, started searching the USPTO database for prior art, before I realized I'd run into FDA bullshit and be stuck for a decade doing clinical trials.

Statue of Limitations

A week later, Toyota would force some over-the-air service patch to all of their vehicles, overriding the custom AC chip, and I was out fifty bucks. Everyone online was saying if you wash your car with Coca-Cola and didn't rinse off the sticky residue, it would prevent the update from happening. This did not work.

No Zodiacs or Almanacs

The Rush song "The Twilight Zone" is far superior to "Roll the Bones" in every way, and this is impressive considering how "Roll the Bones" is basically the best song Rush has ever written. This has been scientifically proven by deep learning computational modeling. (Kingma, Diederik P., and Jimmy Lei Ba. *"From Nome to Rome, boy: A Method for Stochastic Optimization Using a Gradient-based Optimizer in Deep Learning Systems." International Conference on Learning Representations*, 2017.)

Geddy Lee played the bass part on a prototype 7-string bass with an aluminum neck and a mahogany three-piece body, with the strings tuned in an open pentatonic scale, an octave below standard tuning but he played it above the 12th fret. This gave him better tone. He also used a Sansamp.

Rod Serling heard a 22-minute rough cut of the song in 1975 and it gave him a fatal heart attack. His PR people had to cover this up and say it was from habitual smoking, but it's clear this was not true.

The FDA forced the band to cut down the song to under four minutes to avoid mass deaths. Wonder Mike from The Sugarhill Gang heard a bootleg of the extended song, which originally had a seven-minute long rap sequence. He liked the idea so much, two years later he wrote the song "Rapper's Delight" which is often (mistakenly) referred to as the first rap song.

After hearing the song on *2112*, Hoshino Gakki quit his job at the Tokyo Bank and started Ibanez guitar, so he could someday sell extended-scale basses. He later said his life's ambition was to get Geddy Lee to play Ibanez, and after Lee came out with a signature Fender Jazz bass decades later, he committed ritual seppuku and disemboweled himself with a Steve Vai JEM2KDNA guitar headstock. (The JEM2KDNA is a 2000 model with which the red paint in the swirl finish actually contained Steve Vai's blood.)

The only reason the band did not get a Grammy for the song was Barry fucking Manilow and "I Write the Songs." Total bullshit.

The Gamut of Human Disaster, Now Available at Sears

- No more than three members of the Jackson 5 can legally be in a Pizza Hut in Maine at the same time.

- In 1919, the *Flint Journal* became the first US newspaper to experiment with a soup-based broadsheet format. They intended to deliver cans of alphabet soup that contained letters arranged in the form of daily news. This failed, but research led to the development of steel beer cans first released in 1935.

- The United Nations Detention Unit in the Hague Penitentiary Institution's Scheveningen prison currently contains three inmates awaiting execution who were charged with crimes against humanity involving premeditated lawnmower-related injury.

- An anti-Spanish language law passed in Kansas in 2019 accidentally made it illegal to teach algebra in a public school if an equation uses the variable y.

- If the manager of a US bank buys more than ten copies of Steely Dan's 1977 album *Aja*, the Uniform Financial Institutions Rating System will increase the bank's CAMELS rating by two points out of a possible five, usually triggering a listing on the FDIC's problem bank list, indicating the bank may fail in the near future.

- 20% of the Buick LD5 231 V-6s shipped in 1975 were missing a piston.

- There's a company in West Virginia that sells petri dishes of period-accurate staph infection bacteria for use in Civil War re-enactments. Their products killed 27 people in 2023. They were available on Etsy, but their shop got shut down and they had to move to the dark web.

- The corpse of Osama bin Laden is in a storage facility in Vineland, New Jersey. It's the same warehouse that contains the original machinery and recipes used in the initial production of Little Debbie snack cakes.

- Indiana's strategic nacho cheese reserves are locked thirty feet underground in a concrete bunker beneath the mass grave for the victims of Allegheny Airlines Flight 853 in Shelbyville, Indiana.

- Fredrick Dusenberg was killed in the high-speed crash of a prototype passenger car he invented.

- Every Color Me Mine paint-your-own-pottery store keeps an authentic Masamune katana sword in the back room in case shit goes down and the cashier needs a deadly close-quarters weapon. (Because of local laws, many California stores only keep a Taser under the cash register.)

- The Oklahoma constitution specifies that it's required that the government have at least three dozen deviled eggs at every state murder trial. There is an official recipe for the eggs, and it uses yellow mustard because Dijon mustard is too spicy.

- The first person to ever be killed by deorbiting space debris was a vitamin salesman in a house containing at least four million dollars of illegal supplements.

Live Fast, Eat Limestone

The judge speed-ran through seventeen court cases in a row, trying to clear the docket so he could make dollar wing night at the place with the pornographic video trivia game out on Fifth Street. For one case, he sentenced someone to ten years without even hearing the charges first. It resembled the video game tournaments where dudes (always dudes) played *Donkey Kong* at full speed and pressed the switches to jump and move even before the phosphors burned in the screen to show where the characters were, using pure instinct, reacting to patterns with involuntary nervous reactions.

"I'd like to buy my gravestone while I still have the money, before the state takes it all away." A convicted drug-runner gave an impromptu press conference outside the courthouse using a Mr. Microphone and an ancient pink JC Penney jambox. He wore a cheap suit jacket that looked like something the state prison would bury an inmate in. Underneath it he wore a long-sleeve t-shirt for the Florida death metal band Acheron, from their *Satanic Victory* album, the one with the image of a crucified Christ's corpse on the front. A single crew from the local UHF station recorded him with a Quasar camcorder, and a long-hair who did a thrash metal zine and heard about it on the police scanner took notes, just in case the convict went postal and started a mass-murder spree that would make a good death metal song. "I've spent a lot of time at the graveyards next to prisons, and the stones are always bullshit. Cheap rock, uneven grave bases, inscriptions carved out by people who can't even read. Sometimes they don't even have names, only numbers. Fuck that noise. When I die in prison, I want something with a Lamborghini on it, and a solid slogan, like 'Live Fast, Eat Ass' or 'Gas, Grass, or Ass - nobody rides for free.' Maybe a Bruce Lee quote. And after I'm dead, people will visit from around the world to take a shit on my grave, just for LOLs. It worked for GG Allin, right?" The zine dude tried to tell him that the DEA could seize his tombstone in a RICO act thing, but he wouldn't listen. Also the batteries in the jambox died after about seven minutes, and it took 32 D-cells, so this event was done.

An up-and-coming stone-carver in Nevada saw the news segment on a stupid meme site and tried to write the drug dealer in prison to tell him he could totally design the monument. He'd just graduated from a top-tier building arts junior college where he specialized in architectural stone cutting, but couldn't find a job without a union card. (Most funeral homes in Clark County were inexplicably under the Culinary Workers Union Local 226, maybe because they always served food.) His letters never got through. Years before, the dealer legally changed his name to Joey Jailbreak (he was a big Thin Lizzy fan) and all of his mail got automatically tossed by the prison staff, because they assumed he was trying to plot the great escape. (Never go to prison if your last name is Hacksaw or Cocaine. You'll never get your packages.) The cutter later did a full-sized limestone statue of John Jacob Astor around the time the *Titanic* movie came out, but everyone thought it was a bad George Washington, and he ended up throwing it in a river.

* * *

Talking to a kid at Buffalo Wild Wings who lost his brother in college — he was playing Dungeons and Dragons in the steam tunnels under Three Mile Island when it blew up. They never found the body, so the parents buried his dirty laundry in a coffin, a box of sweaty t-shirts and balled-up socks that smelled like a locker room, even with the casket hermetically sealed. "They must have had four hundred pounds of clothes and shoes stuffed in that box. Took ten of us to carry it out of the hearse and throw it in the hole, everyone trying to hold their breath because of the stench. Three people passed out. It was pretty metal."

He half-expected the brother to show up years later, say he wasn't really in the tunnels, and was at a buddy's house listening to Satanic music and looking at *Juggs* magazine when the power plant blew. Or maybe he joined the army without telling anyone and shipped out to Germany, or hid low in a freaky commune in rural Oregon. Something like that, pronounced dead, new start, moved to Alaska to smoke dope and work on shrimp boats — the urban legend job of working in a cannery factory for twenty hours a day at fifteen bucks an hour. That's what the parents hoped, according to the memorial page on Facebook. I looked it up later, killing time at the DMV. His dad posted every day saying how much he missed drinking votka with him. All-caps status updates, of course.

What's the protocol for having a duplicate headstone like that? (Funny that Tom Hanks was the kid that went nuts in that *Mazes and Monsters* disaster of a movie about D&D, and was also the guy in *Cast Away* with the empty grave back home.) Do you have to destroy the old headstone before you add a new one? Can they put a limestone bondo of some sort into the old date and engrave a new one? Do they carve an asterisk next to it? What did they do for Jesus? I don't know how to google this without falling down a grave site k-hole or getting pulled into a religious web page.

* * *

The stonecutter had a brother in the finance department at a Chevy-Isuzu dealership out in Henderson and exclusively worked with college basketball programs, buying cars for recruits under the table. Any time a Big Ten team needed to score a Corvette or an IROC Z-28 for an incoming freshman and hide the paperwork from the NCAA, he was the guy who could hook them up. He also had a side hustle buying back wrecked sports cars and fixing them up with a salvage title for resale, so any time a star quarterback wrapped their Challenger around a tree in a drunk-driving accident, he could quickly repair and turn around the car and make a few bucks.

"I'm just providing a service," he told an NCAA lawyer who was trying to get him drunk at lunch, prying for details on why the UNLV parking lot was full of brand new Corvette C8 ZR1s. "Most of those boys saved up their whole lives for college, and then when they got a scholarship to play ball, they'd blow their school money on a set of wheels. Something like that. Hey man, you looking for a deal on an Isuzu D-Max? Fastest selling mid-size pickup in Kenya. I can get you free clear-coating and everything. Tell 'em Rob sent you!" Luckily the car dealer was so much of an alcoholic, a twelve-drink lunch didn't do anything to him, and he was able to keep his story straight. He told the NCAA stooge that he thought the Final Four was a CIA conspiracy used to cover the fact the government and the Fire Department of Humanity killed Megadeth guitarist Marty Friedman in 1999 and replaced him with a clone, which is why he quit Megadeth and moved to Japan. On the way home, a cop pulled him over and he blew a 0.00 on the breathalyzer even though he drank 14 top-shelf Long Island Ice Teas in under an hour. Two years later, he died in a bizarre above-ground swimming pool accident when he was hit by flying shrapnel from a low-altitude helicopter collision. No idea what his gravestone looked like, although I'd assume his brother hooked him up.

Statue of Limitations

[The UNLV Lied Library Special Collections archive has a copy of Jon Konrath's 2004 book Dealer Wins. It's highly advisable you don't read it, because Jon Konrath is a horrible person. -Ed.]

Dumb story ideas that didn't make it

- A 50,000-word academic review about the time Dokken did a jazz fusion album to celebrate the death of Herbie Hancock.

- Vintage erotica about Lyndon Johnson's fetish for illegal u-turns.

- A detective murder mystery set in London in the 1980s, but every character has primary polydipsia, the mental disorder where you drink too many fluids due to a perceived dry mouth. Princess Diana is giving out bottled water to afflicted people at Trafalgar Square when she is assassinated by an MI6 agent.

- A choose your own adventure book about bowel disorders

- A series of haiku about a serial killer who got a job at McDonald's to hide the dismembered body parts of his victims in the Chicken McNuggets, resulting in a class action lawsuit over the declared percentage of chicken content in advertisements.

- Two men who worked for the government auditing the thickness of printed paper money who start skipping work every day so they can go to a Giant Food grocery store and compulsively masturbate to boxes of Count Chocula in hopes of getting caught.

- The story starts with a man in the booth of a diner, his table full of puke. He's crying, slobbering, re-eating the mostly unchewed meatloaf from the pile of chunder. He screams "I PAID FOR THE WHOLE TRAY OF MEATLOAF, I INTEND TO EAT THE WHOLE TRAY OF MEATLOAF!" It's later revealed that the man is the President of the Solar System and he does this once a year on the anniversary of when he destroyed Earth.

- A guy who used Dr Pepper to sharpen his machete and then invented Juice and moved to Ireland to fight goats.

- A maximalist 7000-page story about a mother of seven at a Chuck-E-Cheese ignoring her kids while she chain-smokes using half a pizza as an ashtray and looks at Tupac autopsy photos on her phone. Six of her kids end up as deadbeats or spend their lives in prison, but one gets a PhD from Stanford in immunology and later proves Jim Henson really died of an anthrax attack.

- A book about an urban legend email forward that's titled *RE: RE: FWD: RE: FWD: FWD: RE: RE: RE:*.

I AM CHARLES FOSTER KANE, AND I'M GONNA GET MEDIEVAL ON YOUR ASS!

Hour four of the Quentin Tarantino remake of *Citizen Kane*, and I prayed to God, Allah, and Satan they would have some kind of *Gone With the Wind*-style intermission so I could take a dump. I accidentally drank a colonoscopy prep phosopho-soda laxative with my chili-dog during the trailers, and the rumbling in my guts told me I was almost out of time. Never go into a Tarantino movie with the slightest chance that you might shit your pants in the next six hours, because you probably will.

The woman next to me in the theater ate a fried ostrich leg she snuck in from the Ost-Fil-A restaurant, a new restaurant that served the biggest chunks of deep-fried flightless bird flesh imaginable to the pro-Jesus, anti-gay crowd imaginable. (Not to be confused with Osto-Fil-A, which is a pro-Jesus store for fetishists who ate from colostomy bags.) The chain closed on Sundays, didn't let women work there, flew a Confederate flag at every store, and all their tables were equipped for motorized wheelchairs. It was basically a license to print money in the south, even before they came out with a *Dukes of Hazzard* emu sandwich.

When not shoving cold, half-coagulated waffle-fries in her gaping maw, she wiped her greasy hands on a knockoff iPad tablet computer, one of those Chinese things you buy at the drug store for $40 and break into a million pieces two hours later. She played a game where you did nothing but click a picture of a dog over and over; each time she clicked, the tinny speaker on the tablet shouted "LOL" over and over. Simply titled *DOG LOL*, this was the most popular game in the world, and they already planned a feature movie based on it. Each time she clicked on it and the dog said "LOL," she said "LOL," and spit food onto the tablet and the seat in front of her, which caused the three-year-old kid she brought to an NC-17 movie that was dropping an f-bomb every two seconds to also say "LOL." She would then slap the kid for talking during the movie and yell "SHUT THE FUCK UP, LOL," and give him more Mountain Dew. I thought she was punctuating the end of her sentences with "LOL" to be ironic or whatever, but it turns out the kid was actually named LOL. Then another dog would pop up, she'd click it, it would say "LOL," she would say "LOL," repeat. I thought about saying something to her, but saw she had a gold-plated AK-47 with a 30-round banana clip sticking out of her fake Dolce handbag, and if I complained about her talking during the movie, a dozen other people would beat me to death for talking during the movie.

At about the five-hour mark, Tarantino had Jedediah Leland burst out of the retirement home holding an M-249 machine gun, shooting from the hip in full-auto mode at a sea of elderly men and women with belt-fed 5.56mm ammunition in 200-round links. He screamed the hard-r n-word over and over inexplicably as the old people geysered blood across the screen. Tarantino wandered into the shot in his usual director cameo, wearing a daishiki and a *Frankenhooker* trucker hat, screaming "THE PROTAGONIST HAS AUTISM! GIVE ME AN OSCAR! THE PROTAGONIST HAS AUTISM! GIVE ME AN OSCAR! NO CGI WAS USED IN THE FILMING OF THIS SCENE! AUTISM! OSCAR! I'M RETIRING AFTER THIS MOVIE, DO IT!"

And then it hit. I rushed from my seat to the bathroom, left behind $74 of snacks and drinks. The intestinal pain was too much; the deluge was about to happen. In the restroom, an elderly Italian man with a flat-top afro used a Braun cordless razor to shave off his eyebrows. "Is that robot thing still on, my man? You a tough guy? I own 47 acres of land in the Florida panhandle and I'm looking to ride a bike across the country next year. It's for charity!" I ignored him, found an empty stall, assumed the position. I hoped a weapons-grade bacteria would kill me, but I knew my estate would only get some free movie coupons out of the deal.

My phone was dead, so I had to read the label on a bottle of Dr. Bronner's soap, for lack of any other literary material. For some unknown reason, the built-in soap dispensers at every sink that auto-dispensed antiseptic gel with motion detectors were long dead, replaced with loose bottles of the Whole Foods natural stuff that would get immediately stolen. The soap had some tirade in two-point type about the Rothschild banking cartel being behind the Mars lander hoax in order to cause brain fog and astigmatism in the general population. I couldn't make the connection, but part of it was that I needed new glasses or bifocals or progressives and I could barely focus on the tiny font. (I guess they got to me.) My near vision suddenly vanished when I turned 40, along with my hairline and half the discs in my spine. I crossed the equivalent of a hundred thousand miles on the odometer of a Ford car, and would spend my free time worrying about how much life I had left and how I wasn't getting shit done anymore.

The soap smelled like a fake candy made out of fruit scrap leftovers given to hippy children who aren't allowed to have sugar. I had some experience in this arena, because my hypochondriac parents thought I was allergic to chocolate for a few years of my childhood, which meant several Easters and Halloweens of horrible carob and beet health store snacks that forever instilled a total hatred of vegetarianism and organic food. (And fuck Peeps. Peeps are bullshit.) The steady diet of sugar-free fake chocolate treats also caused horrible gastric disorder, and I spent most of the first grade on a toilet, memorizing the phone book, for lack of any other reading material.

I don't even know if they still make phone books anymore. I had some strange desire to find one, and read all the non-phone information in the front and back, like the procedures for how to contact the phone company to change services, or the civil defense information on what to do during a nuclear war or large-scale disaster. It might make good meme material, a hyper-focused ironic Tumblr page. Reading these as a kid made me dream of a time when I would have my own full-on panic room, with full airlock, armor plating, oxygen generating gear, air scrubbing fans capable of cleaning biohazards, and of course, an endless supply of chocolate bars, those civil defense corps ones with plain foil wrappers that could survive a nuclear attack.

In Switzerland, there are enough fallout shelters to protect 114% of the Swiss population. Not sure if they overbuilt like that so they could spread out a bit, or if they expect a bunch of unprepared Frenchmen to pop over the border when WWIII starts. Maybe they're predicting a mass weight gain in the future, once they get Taco Bell there. I thought for sure America exceeded that percentage back in the day, two or three shelters per person, just because we're America, god damn it. There would be entire malls underground, for the continuity of society. Fast food outlets would continue to fry onion rings from deep storage for at least ten years. American Gladiator rings would be buried deep under the earth, and government bunkers filled with Cabbage Patch Kids and Atari game systems would keep America prosperous after those 40,000 Soviet warheads rained from the sky.

But that didn't happen, of course. No malls, above or below-ground. The old shelters from the Fifties and Sixties are lost, long since forgotten. No phone books, either. Keep a gun in your dresser and a boat in the back yard, because even a five-minute interruption in power and cable TV will bring on Armageddon in the streets. I lived through two New York blackouts and at least three garbage strikes — I'm a bit of an expert here.

While I was doing my business, one of the theaters had a gunman break into the auditorium and unload a thousand rounds out of an AK-47 into the audience. He somehow managed to miss with every single shot. One person's bag of Jujyfruits got grazed, but it didn't even hit any of the candy, because 90% of that package is air. News channels played the clip from *Pulp Fiction* where the kid unloads a hand cannon into John Travolta and Samuel L. Jackson and misses. It actually turns out the theater gunman was a SAG member, and for some reason related to the new SAG royalty contract, it's cheaper for the news networks to run the clip from the Tarantino movie than the security footage of the shooting.

Someone banged on the stall door. "Can you hurry up, dude? I just ate a box of carob chews and I'm about to die out here, brother." Typical. How much diarrhea will these hippies cause in their lifetime? They should honestly call everything in a health food store "memory food," because you're definitely going to remember it the next morning.

Jon Konrath

The Silver and Gold Manalishi (With the Two Prong Crown)

We tried to send three men to the moon as part of a viral ad campaign for Pepsi, but the rocket blew up on the pad, and the soda manufacturer sued NASA, the NOAA (the explosion was possibly weather-related) and Coca-Cola (who allegedly pumped massive amounts of benzene into the stratosphere to throw off the launch.) The legal battle ran for years, with both Pepsi and Coke conducting massive astroturfing campaigns against each other via cheap ad buys during the off-season. And the sad thing is, it did nothing to boost drink sales, because this was the year Oprah had on a guest that lost a hundred pounds chugging their own piss, so every dumpy housewife in the square states carried a plastic jug of urine with them everywhere, and didn't touch fizzy sugar water or any other fluid.

It's Christmas Eve, and I just got off the phone with my buddy Melvin, who spent an hour talking about how he'd drink Oprah's piss if she paid him enough, but only Fat Oprah because of the urine contaminants from a high-calorie diet. "It's all about the taste. Back when she was pushing 300, her piss was probably 75% saturated fat. Your kidneys can only filter out so much, you know. You want the rich, full body taste of a heavy-calorie piss filled with high-test lipids." I thought about telling him about this art project I once saw where some rich asshole designer distilled his diabetic grandmother's piss and made an artisanal single malt whiskey from it, but I didn't want to encourage him.

[I wish I was making this story up, but it seriously happened. The artist's name was James Gilpin. Look it up. -Ed]

Melvin had to vanish that night, sucked into some family Jesus-based activity, probably a twelve-hour church service where the congregation self-flagellated for not giving enough money to the pastor's annual Lear Jet campaign. My parents were too lazy to bring us to church anymore (which is fine by me, now that I'm a Satanist) and too self-involved to do any family activities with us, so I spent most holidays alone. Looking back, this was ideal during my introverted high school and college years, when I could sit in my basement contemplating Rush albums and binge-watching zombie movies. But later as an adult, that pleasure/dopamine bar was set so high, nothing really worked anymore, and I spent my solo holidays contemplating where exactly I went wrong.

When I said "we" sent someone to the moon, by the way, I meant the collective "we" and not like my company or me personally. I mean, I pay taxes, so ultimately I'm fiscally responsible for some fraction of the space program, but my return would cover like the cost of a single Space Shuttle toilet seat, if that. I've never done anything worthwhile in my life, except maybe that one time I donated fifty bucks to a guy who needed a liver transplant, and the surgery actually happened, the new liver took, and he did fine until like ten years later when he got in a drunk driving accident, ran into a streetcar at full speed during a police pursuit, and got internally decapitated. (They were able to put his liver in someone else though, and it wasn't completely burned out from his deep relapse into alcoholism. So partial credit there, I guess.)

With nothing to do except sit around listening to Judas Priest records backwards, I decided to bundle up and walk to the corner store for some nachos and a corn dog. The secret to the gas station nacho/corn dog combo is to put about a gallon of nacho cheese in the tray before you add the chips, then put down a layer of chips, add a top layer of cheese, then dip the 'dog in cheese when you've finished eating the measly seven chips they give you for $2.97. It was about forty out, but a windless night, no traffic on the road, complete seclusion.

I made the walk with no problems, contemplated the nothingness on the moonlit night and felt almost calm and at peace. But when I got there, they were out of corn dogs, out of cheese, and the cashier wouldn't sell me anything with caffeine because he was a secret Mormon or something. They also weren't taking credit cards. I ended up buying a Milky Way bar with the emergency two-dollar bill in my wallet, just to have the energy to walk back home, but Milky

Statue of Limitations

Way is a bullshit candy bar made for people who don't have the balls to eat a Snicker's.

Terms and Conditions

A trio of stealth bombers made a low-altitude pass over the soccer field, then banked over the horizon and looped back, dropping tens of thousands of pounds of Joint Direct Attack Munition GPS-guided bombs on the guy dressed as the Statue of Liberty in the parking lot of the Modell's sporting goods store. (President's Day sale: 15% off all trampolines in stock, no rainchecks. Free cotton candy, bring the kids.) There was some anti-calisthenics movement going on in the Dark State Department, and a group of NSA operatives in a trailer at Peterson AFB were shit-posting thousands of times an hour on every social media account, endless fake news stories about how ISIS converts were bulking up with those monkey bar exercises in the desert, and True Americans needed to eat more cheese. They were also manipulating dairy futures. They bought every option on the open market for the Kraft corporation, and were waiting to press the button and cash out big.

The planes floated overhead, then suddenly dropped nose-down in a high-G maneuver, a frantic turn-and-burn gone sideways. The lead pilot wasn't paying attention, trying to answer a text while flying, and the trio of planes collided in mid-air. Pieces of the burning jets plummeted into a TGI Friday's parking lot on the outskirts of the airport, a four-billion dollar thunderstorm of jet fuel and lethal chunks of shrapnel falling from the sky. The PR wonks in the White House would have to put their idiot press secretary of the week out on the West Wing podium and have him spout out an hours' worth of flat earth theory and anilingus limericks as a distraction technique while the bean-counters figured out what vital social program would have to get cancelled so they could afford some new planes.

The stealth bomber pilots all managed to safely eject before the planes fireballed into the mini-mall. They parachuted into a Jeep/Subaru dealership with a 0% down/0% interest for 36 months special, making a rough landing in front of the certified preowned light sport/utility vehicle line. The customer service team brought the plane crew members into the pre-sales offices, where Dale the Finance Guy waxed poetic on the durability of the Subaru opposed-four engine, then bled the new customers with extended warranties, dealer-installed trailer hitches, and overpriced undercoating options.

"I can get you that 0% down, but let me tell you a story about my uncle Lenny, who was a Mennonite missionary in the Congo. Got beheaded by a tribe of evangelical Janis Joplin fans who were pissed at the government over their NCAA men's basketball bracket. Don't know why someone would make the Mississippi Valley State Delta Devils their top pick, but no wonder they were upset. Uncle Lenny used to mail me boxes of religious peanut brittle, and I had a lot of dental work that prevented me from eating it, so I'd melt that shit down and use it to power a quarter-scale steam locomotive around my back yard. I used to ride that damn thing day and night, blasting Krokus tapes on my jam box. They later came out with that Steam video game platform, and I was convinced for a while that I could gin up a good trademark lawsuit, but I guess it was just low blood sugar, hypoglycemia. Really, I should have been eating that peanut brittle! I could have melted it down, drank the raw peanut juice, why not? But I had diabetes and they had to saw off one of my legs. It's wood now, wood! Check this shit out..."

He pulled off his fake leg, rapped it on the table like a Sammy Sosa corked baseball bat. The stump end of the appendage was drenched in foul-smelling sweat and pus, and resembled a wooden spittoon. "This baby's made out of pure mahogany, with rosewood inserts. You can't even import that shit anymore, something about the god damned rainforests. Now imagine I'm walking down the road, and that wooden leg flies off, and you're driving by, and it scratches the hood of your car. That's like 40% of the retail value of your vehicle, up in smoke!" He pulled out a small square of sheet metal, finished in the same color as a new car, but with a deep gouge in the middle, like someone tried to cut it in half with a table saw. "Ouch! Right? But I can put on this clear coating for only $4995 that will protect your hood. It's made out of chopper blades, the same stuff the black helicopters use when they're violating your civil rights. I mean, it's the same laminated covering as chopper blades.

I'm not saying your car is gonna fly, heh. Now you guys are stealth bomber pilots — you know the value of a good composite material. But your planes cost a billion dollars each. This is less than five thousand dollars! You can't even buy a seat cover for a stealth bomber for five grand. This is less than five grand! It's $4995! And we can even finance it for you. It's less than a cup of coffee every hour for the lifetime of your car!"

The dealership service employees, crazed on energy drinks and sexual repression from a recent harassment reprogramming session, were convinced that the airmen, who wore flight suits with no identifying patches or labels, were the secret Zionist Occupational Group soldiers detailed in the latest *Infowars* episode. After Dale the Finance Guy wasn't able to sell them thousand-dollar cargo nets, they dragged the men into a back service bay used to wax and detail new inventory, and utilized enhanced interrogation techniques to find out more information, blasting Jeep ads at deafening volumes, then waterboarding the pilots with five-gallon Poland Springs water cooler bottles, until four of the six confessed to crimes against humanity. A guy named Johnny Reb screamed "TELL US ABOUT YOUR PATCHES!" for hours, not getting any information whatsoever. (These pilots won't talk — they go to a special training in Arizona for exactly this type of situation.)

Before the stealth bomber pieces completely immolated outside, rubber-neckers circled the Circuitry City parking lot, looking for a good piece of composite radar-absorbent material to drag home as a souvenir. An old woman in a Gorguts shirt ran around in circles, her head impaled with a piece of titanium driven through her skull sideways like a Steve Martin fake arrow. People grabbed up sizable chunks of EMP-resistant MIL-STD-1750A avionics computers and crash-survivable memory units from the flight recorders, and hauled them to their 4x4 trucks, so they could bring them back to their man caves and eat tater tots smothered in nacho cheese while watching that new show on the history channel about how aliens helped the Confederate army win in an alternate history timeline. It was sponsored by Cialis and the new Monster Truck Network.

#ColchicineLifestyle

It was the anniversary of some famous massacre, or maybe a race riot or worker uprising, something they remove from high school history books and you have to find out later from a sixth-year junior who smokes way too much weed in your college dorm, a guy with black light posters and a stupid Bob Marley hat allegedly made out of hemp who rips off Howard Zinn and tries to bang age-inappropriate freshmen girls who didn't know any better. (I went to high school in Indiana, and we didn't even cover the Civil War. And my teacher told us that the Great Depression was a hoax.) Everyone was changing their Facebook profile picture to have a picture of a black flag on it, and for a few minutes, I thought maybe ISIL had won the war, or recruited Benedict Cumberbatch or Dale Earnhardt and caused everyone to flip allegiances. Or maybe Henry Rollins and Greg Ginn finally reconciled and got the band back together, not that there's any shortage of Black Flag pseudo-reunions these days. I never pay attention to this shit, and every time I do, it only results in high blood pressure, increased stress, and I end up re-buying a band's entire discography because they remastered it again.

Every cable channel on the hospital waiting room TV bolted to the wall fixated on the historical non-event, in an effort to create content, showing the same four stock photos and scrolling through a generic set of facts and figures that anyone could find on wikipedia. (Pro tip: bring your own universal remote everywhere, so you can turn off Fox News in airports.) Even the stupid house-flipper channel interrupted their regular programming of installing granite countertops and stainless-steel appliances to run a loop of prefabricated nothing-news narrated by Mark McGrath.

"Saw a guy in the emergency room who had a telephone pole sticking out of his gut." Melvin loved to hang out at the hospital too much, because he couldn't afford Netflix. He chewed on the leading edge of a cold calzone as big as his head, which looked like it contained tater tots and strips of fat, rubbery bacon that wasn't cooked enough. "They use these flip-over cannons in stunt cars. Launches a chunk of utility pole out of the bottom of the car with a big ol' gunpowder explosion. Dude was trying to fuck a stunt car on the Universal backlot, accidentally fired the damn thing through his abdomen. I don't know what they do for that. Stem cells, maybe. Stem cells and leeches. Maybe a laser, too. Or an abs transplant. They do those yet? When I filled out my organ donor card, I just donated my dick."

An ad played for an insurance company, an elderly man beating a cartoon rattlesnake with a golf club, while a voice-over said "big time!" over and over. (It wasn't the Peter Gabriel song.) They ran some variation of the ad every commercial block: it would change from an old man to a

Mexican woman, then from a golf club to a piece of lumber, then the "big time!" slogan became a song about tacos. I had a feeling this was an A/B test of some sort, like maybe they were changing the 800 numbers, measuring who reacted to what. They also gave no details on the actual insurance product, probably to avoid some truth-in-advertising law. I didn't even know people bought insurance anymore. I thought it was all "Jesus take the wheel" and filing for bankruptcy online in these parts.

I gave up on the waiting room. I was there for an asthma attack, or maybe it was gout, I don't remember. Maybe both. (A healthy dose of Predisone cures either one. Also, I threw the gout thing in here because it seems like I talk about gout in every book I write. I did a book reading this year and randomly pulled five or six stories to read, and it turns out every single one mentioned gout. I should rebrand myself as the gout writer. Maybe I can get a sweet influencer deal with a comfortable shoe company. Not Crocs. Fuck Crocs.) I wandered the hallways of the hospital, looking for something to do, or maybe a rogue oncologist or dermatology intern who would write me a script for some steroids or maybe painkillers. I somehow wandered into an operating theater, and nobody seemed to care or stop me to gown up and put on a mask.

"420 blaze it," the surgeon said, before firing up the cutting torch. "LOL, fire." He haphazardly burned the face off a brain-dead suicide victim, probably to sell it on eBay to another transplant clinic. The whole time, a nurse helped him vape some wicked weed through his surgical mask. Ever since Gwenyth Paltrow got a new face sewn on to replace her original one that was destroyed by some hippy cure involving snake venom and organic battery acid, every mommyblogger on the planet wanted their doctor to find a cadaver on the down-low. Yoga classes looked like a demented *Texas Chainsaw Massacre* sequel these days. It would almost be cool if it wasn't.

"Hey man, can you transplant the abs off a dead dude? Like slice off the six-pack and glue it back on another person?"

"Hmm, I haven't thought about that," the surgeon said. The nurse held up a surgical bong, and he took a long hit through his face mask. The mask had a special port that he could hook up to the smoking device, like a surgical port but for smoke. It probably cost $47,000 per disposable mask. "Might be a good procedure for a plastic surgeon, though. Instant six-pack abs. The hard part is lining up donors. Maybe we could 3-D print some. You care if I use that one?"

"Be my guest." I'd long since given up on trying to patent these million-dollar ideas. I think that surgical bong was my idea and NASA stole it. Back in 1987, I had the entire idea of Amazon dot com written down on the back of an Ozzy album, and would probably have enough money to buy my own aircraft carrier if I could find it. Anyway.

I watched the operation for a minute, and caught some secondhand off the guy's medical-grade sativa, but it was boring, and I didn't want to stick around for hours while a team of organ harvesters ran train on the corpse, scooping out heart, lungs, liver, kidneys, everything down to his dick and balls for resale. I went back to find Melvin and get a ride to Denny's, but he either left or was institutionalized, so I had to take a Lyft and listen to some ex-professional wrestler ramble on about constitutional law for twenty minutes while we were stuck in traffic from the weekly anti-GMO protest. "Some day, we're going to be able to legally run these fuckers down, and I'm going to get a snow plow put on my Suzuki Samurai." Big time! Big time!

When Dream and Dumb Unite

She told me she was having a topless barbecue and that she was in love with me and I should come over and bring chips. She was completely drunk, and I'm obviously stupid, so with little hesitation, I bought a bag of Ruffles and a bag of Doritos, because I didn't know what kind of party this would be. Her apartment was about a dozen miles away, and I didn't have a car, so I had a long night of walking ahead of me. The road east of town was more of a county highway, with no sidewalks or shoulders, and any time a rare car passed by at high speed, the passenger typically yelled a homophobic slur at me, or maybe threw an empty bottle at my head. And my walkman batteries slowly died about two tapes into the hike. Luckily one of the tapes was Godflesh - *Streetcleaner*, which sounds even better at half speed.

I tried to think of some mental game to play while I made the death march in the darkness, a way to steer my internal monologue away from the obvious thought that I should probably just lay down in traffic and let a DUI in a truck end this. Everyone says walking is mindfulness, but that's bullshit designed to sell app subscriptions. This part of the world looked like if they built an artificial golf course on the surface of the moon and then abandoned it before PGA certification. There were nominally a few farms and giant

McMansions on hundred-acre plots, places with 17 bedrooms and 23 bathrooms that were built during a housing bubble and would need to be torn down in 2008 because of black mold and sick house syndrome and people committing suicide from their upside-down mortgages.

I brainstormed the most extravagant plumbing features I could add to a house like this, probably thinking specifically about plumbing because I was dying of thirst. I imagined a "deluge toilet," a WC that could purge its contents with a rainforest storm of ten thousand gallons of water for no reason other than wasting ten thousand gallons of water every time you take a crap (20 or 30,000 if you eat a lot of fiber and took a two- or three-flusher). It would be something that rich people love to brag about, and it wouldn't waste that much water given most of these houses sat empty for tax purposes, and if you had 17 bathrooms and avoided Taco Bob, you're probably only taking a dump in each toilet maybe twice a month.

It took me about five hours to walk to the girl's apartment. By the time I arrived, she'd already been hauled off to the county hospital to get her stomach pumped two hours before. They put her on a 48-hour hold for trying to punch a nurse, and she'd manage to stretch that into a three-month bit, then got shuffled back to her parents and spent the rest of her life drifting in and out of institutions. Her roommate, this ROTC-looking woman with a crewcut and bigger biceps than my thighs, told me it might be better if I never talked to her again. Agreed. I didn't want to wake up in a burning bed three dates from now because I said I liked Coke instead of Pepsi.

It's odd I can't even remember her name now. Nadine? Colleen? Collette, maybe. Another two-dimensional memory from my frantic desire to fill The Wound with someone else, something else. A problem as a cure. I did this so much back then, and of course it never took. At some point, one of these things hurt me so much, I had the stupid idea to write books instead, and here we are. I'm probably 500 short stories deep right now, and half of them are about how I couldn't get laid in the Nineties, which ended up being far more productive than the 21st century. (The other half of my writing output is about diarrhea. Or is diarrhea. At least nobody writes reviews of my stuff anymore.)

Dying of thirst, I walked to a gas station a quarter-mile up the road, called my friend Peggy to beg for a ride home. She said she'd come get my sorry ass once she finished her episode of COPS. I ate both party-size bags of chips in the parking lot, then went inside the mini-mart to get a drink and something more substantial to actually eat, since I missed dinner over this stupid quest, and probably burned ten pounds of weight marching across town in the August heat. Also, try eating two large bags of chips without drinking anything. I think that's technically a war crime.

Inside the store, the place also sold bait and fishing equipment. I guess it was close enough to the lake that they got anglers looking for supplies. They also — completely un-related — sold equipment to grow weed indoors: hydroponic setups, lights, various chemicals and fertilizers and trellises and growing medium. They didn't say it was for growing weed, but it had that "for tobacco use only" vibe to it, and nobody invests in ten thousand dollars of fancy lights just to grow a few tomatoes they could buy from a roadside farmer stand for two bucks.

I know too many of my stories are about grocery stores and convenience stores and 7-Elevens and Village Pantry convenience marts. (A little wild card for you Midwestern-ers...) But I never go anywhere else anymore. I've been locked in my house for the last year, but even before that forced isolation, the regular rotation was Target, Panera, CVS, and the gas station. Yeah, I could have spent the pan-demic watching Rick Steeves documentaries on PBS, learn-ing the ins and outs of 163 different countries and writing about the intricacies of travel in 18th century Belarus. But I didn't, so here we are.

I'll cut to the chase and say the convenience store had a single fridge case that said "pop" above it, and the cans of Coke inside said "New Coke" on them, meaning they were at least a decade old and probably nothing but a thick sludge of rust and mold. The same fridge that held the "pop" also contained a wall of plastic containers of earthworms. I de-cided not to buy anything, and sat outside by the gas pumps, my mouth coated with a solid poultice of Frito-Lay sodium.

Maybe they had a garden hose I could drink from. GAR-
DEN HOSE.

Peggy showed up in her car, a mid-eighties Toyota Supra
in two-tone brown with rust highlights. It was supposed to
be all fast and cool, but it made this horrible screeching
sound any time the car did anything except sit perfectly still.
I think it was something about polyurethane bushings or an
overly fucked-out suspension. It sounded like every joint in
the car was designed to make loud noises like a haunted
house ride, and made me think the whole thing was going to
fall apart at any moment. (My own body has a similar problem, but I can't order replacement parts direct from Japan.)

"Get in. There's a COPS marathon on and I need to get
home before I miss another episode."

"Did they taze anyone yet?"

"Of course they fucking tazed someone. Why do you
think I watch it? Now tell me about the disaster of a chick
you didn't fuck so I can make fun of you for the next
month."

* * *

Peggy was just a friend, and despite telling me "we're just
friends and I'd never fuck you" like six times an hour for our
entire friendship, she wrote me a giant letter ten years later
saying she totally wanted to fuck me and was constantly giving me the green light, and I was a fucking idiot for never

picking it up, because I was in a huge drought the entire summer we hung out, and she was constantly doing stuff like "accidentally" walking in the room naked or "accidentally" dumping a bottle of wine on my lap so I had to take off my pants and she could wash them and "accidentally" grabbing my dick and putting it in her mouth. I probably should have fucked her but I chickened out. I guess it was all ambiguous to me, or maybe it's some half-autistic behavior of mine. And then when I called her after getting that letter, she told me she was now really into Jesus, and was in some Amway-based evangelical church and really wanted to help me be my own boss and enter the kingdom of heaven. I imagined the whole blowjob thing was off the table, but hell, maybe the MLM was a green light too. I never know.

* * *

A week later, bought a case of *Paranormal Activity 17* camping food for cheap at Big Lots. I don't camp and am not into horror movies, especially the ones with endless money-grab sequels, but the whole box was $4.97, and it said it had 21 complete meals in it. Maybe I'll eat them if there's another great blackout or mass-terrorism event again. At least the trip wasn't a total loss. I went to the Big Lots because someone told me they were still selling Surge soda, which they were not. I really needed some Surge soda, because it was the only thing that helped me write. Well, Surge soda and Reese's peanut butter cup miniatures, the ones wrapped in gold foil.

And Provigil tablets, ground up into a dust and snorted every three minutes.

What was that soda with the weird little orbs floating in it? Orbital? Orbit? Orbits? I used to shoplift all my extreme satanic metal from a shop called Orbit Records, but they're probably long gone. The drink though: little gel bubble things floated in the bottle, looked like drinking a lava lamp. I never tried it, no idea what it tasted like. It was all weird fruity flavors, I think. Peach, mango. I hate any artificial orange flavor, probably because of the fake orange penicillin syrup I got constantly as a kid, and it turns out I'm allergic to penicillin. I just remember going to the store and shaking the fuck out of the drink bottles, trying to get the bubbles to break into little pieces, and nothing worked.

I had to look this up just now, and it was called Orbitz. Orbitz, I thought that was a travel agency? Also Big Lots — or their parent company — bought Kay-Bee toy store in the nineties, then ended up selling it to Mitt Romney and his band of assholes so they could drive it into the ground, Goodfellas-style. Also, Mihajlo Petrović from Serbia was the second military pilot ever to be killed in the line of duty. I don't know who was first. He encountered some high wind when he was cruising at about 2500 feet, and fell out of the plane. No seat belts back then, I guess. How did I get from soda to the Serbian air force? This is why I need so much Surge to keep on track with my writing.

I was trying to think of a better way of writing three-dimensionally that week. I found this artist on Instagram who did giant drawings in intricate detail, on sheets of paper that were like eight or ten feet square. They were all carefully inked, which was insane. I'd get an hour into it and completely fuck up, or my pen would explode, and I'd have to start over. Anyway, I wanted to do something similar, but couldn't think of a form or method to do it in. Gregory Corso did this for a minute with his poems typed to look like an atomic bomb mushroom cloud. And I guess Raymond Federman did something similar with *Double or Nothing*. But I wanted more, and couldn't think of how. Isn't this the kind of shit hypertext was supposed to solve?

I almost forgot, but that Big Lots had remaindered copies of the first Dream Theater album, first pressing, only 97 cents each. I went back a week later, and the entire store was gone, shut down, the signage removed, everything inside vanished, the interior stripped down to bare studs. I went into the liquor store next door and asked if they knew what happened, and the lady behind the register said the Big Lots owner fucked the wife of a district manager or something, so the home office showed up and fired everyone, shuttered the whole damn thing, just to prove a point. Big Lots is a family company. No orgies, wife-swapping, or cuckolding, even if it's off the clock.

* * *

Dream Theater is a good example of The Wound and why, aside from chasing women to fix me, I'd fall down these endless rabbit holes of collectorism. I currently own 439 Dream Theater albums, and probably haven't seriously listened to any of them in a quarter-century. Their drummer bootlegs all their shows and sells CD-Rs of them from his basement, and of course I buy all of them. I don't know what this will solve in my life, because the more I buy, the less dopamine is released. I have bought 22 Dream Theater albums or bootlegs this month, and I can't even tell you who's playing keyboards at the moment. I don't care. I don't need this. But I need this.

I found the woman online. Twice widowed, six kids, selling Christian CBD oil out of a truck in New Mexico. I thought about dropping her a line, but I can only hate myself so much.

Surge Country

Another Surge story: Me and Virgil cruised the mini-marts in a hundred-mile radius in his beaten-up jeep, looking for the one magical gas station that might still have Surge soda. (This was after the supply had run out, but long before they briefly rebooted it.) That fully-loaded citrus elixir, a magic mix of caffeine and terror, propelled me through life for years before suddenly vanishing from most stores. Just one fix, I told myself. I needed to avoid sleep, stay awake forever, stop the nightmares. Eventually we'd find some backwater store hung off the side of an illegal chop shop that didn't report their stock back to the Coca-Cola mothership and hung onto a few loose cases. Until then, the same Tool bootleg played through the tape deck for hours, echoing over the sound of wind in the doorless, topless jeep, driving around in circles like a bad video game.

Virgil's name was Virgil "Gus" Griswald. He hated the name Gus, even though his entire family called him that, because he thought astronauts were all assholes. He also disliked the name Virgil, but as an adult, he finally just gave up and owned it. When I met him as a kid, he tried to get everyone to call him Nitro, but every time the teacher would call attendance, she'd call him Virgil and it quashed that nickname. Virgil wanted to become an NFL quarterback, but never played football in school, didn't even like watching games, and if he took the Wonderlic, he'd probably get a rating so low, he couldn't get a job as the stadium janitor in charge of puke-mopping at Lincoln Financial Field in Philadelphia. I still hung out with him regularly for no good reason. Shared history, I guess.

Every time I slept, I had a nightmare I was a realtor who didn't work on commission, and had to sell my old house to a Pakistani family with seven kids, and explain to them why a life-sized plastic Santa Claus was hanging from the forty-foot TV antenna on the side of the tri-level. First I had to explain what a TV antenna was, since everybody used cable or just stole TV shows off the internet — nobody remembered the days of a spaceship-shaped cluster of aerial wiring you had to turn with a motor box to get channel 46 to pull in with no snow. I knew with each round of clarification about the antenna situation, I was taking another thousand dollars of value off the house. I only want to answer yes or no to every question for the rest of eternity. Live life like it's a deposition. Anything else is frustration and doom.

Santa flashback: one time I went on a first date with a woman and found out an hour into an expensive dinner that she would only fuck Salvation Army Santas. I considered the logistics of maybe buying a fat suit and a stick-on beard, but I knew I did not have the confidence to pull it off. Also unsure of the religious angle, like if the Salvation

Army makes you take some kind of Christian loyalty oath. No second date, of course.

Back in the dream — I got through another round of endless explanation about the antenna and forced them to sign the thousand pages of mortgage papers, then had to cut down the Santa, drag it and the rest of the old stuff out of the house and into the back yard and burn it. The giant Magnavox TV, bigger than a coffin and made of the same heavy wood, exploded tube by tube in the bonfire, sounding like a barrage of machine gun fire. Something would happen — Andre the Giant explaining to me how to use the GPS in my rental car, or a young Charlie Manson at a bus stop killing ants with a microscope — and I'd be back selling the goddamn house again, *Groundhog Day*-style, except I'd never get to fuck Andie MacDowell. Sleep was no longer an option.

[I recently found out that they sell Urge in Norway, which is pretty much the same thing as Surge, but who gives a shit at this point, we're all going to die.]

Orem Chipotle

Johnny from accounting won a year's supply of frozen corn dogs from some feat of strength at the county fair. I'm not sure how that would work — like do they average out that you're going to eat one a day, and give you a crate of 365 and call it even? Is it just a figure of speech, and they give you like six or eight boxes? Or do you get some sort of golden ticket you can present to any cashier and get as much as you want? If they were fresh out of the fryer at a shitty food truck and I had proper ketchup coverage, I'm certain I could eat twenty or so in a single sitting. The only problem is there's no good way to cook a frozen corn dog. Any microwave attempt results in them splitting in half, the inside turning to beef jerky. The oven takes hours, once you preheat and everything. I guess you could buy your own fryer and run a second pass on them, but if I installed a home fryer, I'd also need to put in double doors so I could ever get out of the house again.

I've seen a similar card thing in action. One time, I ran into Iggy Pop at a Chipotle in Orem, Utah. He had a "black card" from Chipotle corporate, which gave him unlimited everything at any Chipotle restaurant. I guess they used a quote from the song "I Wanna Be Your Dog" on the side of a drink cup, and he got paid with free Chipotle for life. He wasn't actually eating that day — I mean, you don't get an eight-pack like that by plowing through six burritos a day — but he got a gallon of queso blanco, poured it all over his chest, then broke a bottle of beer and started cutting himself with the glass. I had the burrito bowl.

(Orem is the original home of WordPerfect software. Satellite Software International (SSI) had their original offices in the basement of a city office building. Fun fact: the very first tech job I ever had was teaching people WordPerfect 5.1 at a commuter campus in 1990. And one of the first things I ever published was an article in the school newspaper about the rampant computer virus problem on campus, and that people needed to stop booting the lab computers from floppy disk. Every single person involved is now replying in all caps on Facebook about AI slop articles ginned up by bot farms in Nigeria talking about how socialists are taking over our McDonald's restaurants because Heinz ketchup is woke now.)

I bought a monthly pass to JetBlue to make regular visits to a girlfriend in Buffalo, New York, but we broke up immediately after I got out of the cancellation window. I kept the pass, because I liked the idea of randomly flying places, and thought about taking haphazard weekend trips to Florida or Vegas or whatever, or maybe just going back and forth between JFK and Salt Lake City as many times as possible in a weekend, so I could write uninterrupted and eat their free snacks. When I couldn't deal with a lack of air conditioning in my apartment, I used to do the same thing with the subway, shuffling between my place in Astoria and Coney Island, the furthest station south of me on the BMT line. The JetBlue thing was a nice idea, but they only flew to like three cities at the time, and they were all cities so horrible, the local government was trying to pay people to move there.

I know I've written about this a dozen times, but I often thought about how hard it would be to ride every single MTA train line from end to end. I don't know if it's possible in a day, or how exactly you'd handle the exchanges. Probably ride to Times Square and then ride half of each line in each direction, so you could go out and then back. I don't know if that's cheating, and it might take days. There's 665 miles of track total. Also, not sure how the bathroom situation would work, given that there are 150 stations with bathrooms and 149 of them are currently locked. The other one is a literal death sentence.

That weekend, I booked a last-minute flight to Buffalo, checked a disassembled bicycle in a cardboard box as my luggage, and found a cheap hotel not far from the airport. (Dick Road, lol.) There was a Tim Horton's, a 7-Eleven, and a Wegman's within walking distance, although I wouldn't consider that part of town very walkable. (There were sidewalks, but good luck ever getting a car to stop when you tried to make a break for it at a crosswalk.) I had no idea what else to do there, which left me all the time in the world to write, and of course that meant I had no ideas whatsoever.

The corn dog thing had me thinking about how many bars of soap I used a year, how the size of a hotel bar of soap compared to a full bar, and how many hotel visits I'd have to make a year to completely stop buying soap for the rest of my lifetime. Then I remembered I hate hotel soap. And now, you can't even buy bars of soap half the time.

A bad rower blames the oar

- A booth at the mall offering to dislocate your shoulder for five bucks.

- A hipster who looks like Timothy McVeigh in a tie-dye shirt telling two girls at a pretzel stand that he used to load nuclear weapons onto Huey Cobra choppers in the Army. The Army hasn't flown the Huey since before he was born, and they never carried nuclear bombs. This does not get him laid as planned.

- The weatherman on the Channel 5 news brings a live alligator to his weather report because he's a huge University of Florida fan, and it bites off his arm on live TV.

- The town starts a large marketing campaign (TV and newspaper ads, social media posts, press conferences) announcing that due to budgetary cuts, all active shooter incidents must happen between 10:00 AM and 2:00 PM Monday through Friday.

- Criterion announces a three-DVD Criterion Edition release of *The Jerky Boys: The Movie*, with a commentary track by Noam Chomsky and Tom Brokaw. It only sells five copies, and three of them were bought by Brokaw.

- The price of gas goes up to over ten dollars a gallon. It's later found out that two of the leading manufacturers of gas pumps manipulated prices to make four-digit fuel price displays obsolete and force gas stations to buy new signs.

- Omaha Steaks announces a meat-based meat substitute for people who don't want to eat vegetables but want to use a reconstituted meat-like product to make their friends think they care about the environment.

- The gun industry's lobbyists manage to ban all protective regulations from swimming pools, so more children will die of swimming pool-related accidents than handguns.

- Microsoft buys a space rocket company that launches 4000 web servers to run autonomously on the surface of Mars, so they can legally say that Bing is the best search engine on the planet, but not specify which planet.

- The President of the American Girl Dolls corporation goes on the Geraldo show and says the company is releasing a communist state of Democratic Kampuchea doll, because the company fully supports the Pol Pot Cambodian regime. Geraldo is not wearing a shirt and has a .45 pistol strapped to his thigh. The two-hour special is sponsored by Quizno Subs.

- The year's most popular porn video is a portly naked woman in a motel, riding a Sybian sex toy and playing a Nuno Betancourt double-neck guitar. It was filmed on a VHS-C camcorder, and had "12:00 1/1/80" flashing in the lower corner. The motel has an oil painting on the wall of Pope John Paul riding a jet ski in heaven, surrounded by dolphins. Ten minutes into the video, a guy appears, sporting the top gun spiked haircut and a pair of Oakley's. He starts talking about Otis Spunkmeyer baked goods then has a fatal aneurysm.

- Until they offer cream cheese as a topping, Wetzel's Pretzel is an inferior mall pretzel experience.

What We Talk About When We Talk About Sodium Hypochlorite

I eat less than an hour before swimming. I don't care; I can't swim. I just stand in the water and pretend. I'm not scared of drowning or anything like that. I just refuse to learn because my parents spent a decade trying to teach me. When I was a kid, they enrolled me in swimming lessons, and I spontaneously caught leprosy the night before the first class. The second time, the instructor (who was named Chuck Bowler and looked like an extra from *Dazed and Confused*) divided us into five levels of proficiency, but he had to create an extra level zero just for me because I was so inept in the water. I hung onto the side in the shallow end of the heavily-chlorinated olympic-sized pool and tried to kick and paddle without hitting my feet on the bottom, which I constantly did. I would mostly just splash water for a half-hour, then take a twenty-minute shower to try and scrub away the chlorine damage.

The pool was so chlorinated, you could bring a chunk of ham or turkey lunchmeat and stick it to the tile wall, and within an hour, it would be completely dissolved. They had to close it a few years later, because the bleach had actually eaten away the concrete structure and was destroying the water table of the city. When they tried to build a new pool, the EPA declared the entire school a superfund site and built a two-billion dollar sarcophagus on top of it like it was a decommissioned nuclear reactor. Everyone in town bitched about government interference, while simultaneously making bank on the biggest make-work project in the state's history.

"You know Chuck Bowler died in a bank robbery?" Me and Lars sat in a diner that looked like the one in the opening scene of *Pulp Fiction*. I'm fine with eating bacon, though. And my wallet doesn't say anything on it. I no longer like logos or slogans on any of my clothes or accessories. If you want me to advertise for you, let me send you a rate card. I'm not doing it for free.

"I don't blame him. School gym teachers don't make that much money."

"He wasn't robbing the bank. They had him assassinated, made it look like he died from a poisoned hot dog, but it all came out when the bank went under in 2008. He used to scuba dive in that pond next to the Wokaihwokomas Zoo, the one where people would make a wish and throw in their change. He'd rake the bottom for coins and bring them to the bank every month for beer money. They were sick of him bringing in a thousand pounds of wet, mossy, unrolled coins every month, so they ordered the hit. Why didn't you hear about all of this? It was on Facebook."

"It's not like I set google alerts on my grade-school gym teachers." I used to set them on ex-girlfriends, at least the ones with uncommon names. I briefly dated a woman named Kelly English, and that sure didn't work out search-wise. Neither did any of the alerts for exes who got married and changed their name, which was almost all of them. I think the only useful result from that was the time someone from a decades-ago three-dates-and-you're-out tryst went Ambien driving with her eight kids in their Subaru and ran *Blues Brothers*-style through an Illinois mall. The car landed upside-down in a Spencer's Gifts store. Luckily, none of the kids were hurt — all the fake rubber vomit in the Spencer's cushioned the crash somewhat, and the mall was 90% empty. I hoped I would not somehow get deposed as a character witness on that one, but that was a brief period of time when the alumni association could not find me.

Our waitress said she used to be the CEO of Priceline.com, but got fired by William Shatner because she didn't speak Esperanto. She was also a horrible waitress, and kept bringing me cups of coffee with ice in them because I wanted a Coke no ice. Every time I told her that's not what I ordered, she came back twenty years later with the same thing.

"I think they hire only people who can't read, like as a tax break," Lars said. "They should get a cash register with only pictures of food on it, like McDonald's."

"I think that's an urban legend, but I haven't eaten at McDonald's in like ten years, so who knows."

Statue of Limitations

Situs inversus is not a black metal band

The Subway cashier with the Eighties-as-fuck hair stared at me through her greasy LensCrafter plastic bifocal glasses, like I just took a Satanic shit in the middle of her Sunday school class. She took her Subway Artist credentials too seriously, like a watercolor hobbyist who sold a crying clown paint-by-number at a charity auction for twenty bucks and let it go to her head, getting stupid-looking business cards made at VistaPrint and wearing a beret at all times, even in the bathtub.

I'd been holding up the whole line, searching my George Costanza wallet for a frequent-flyer rewards card, but fucking shoot me, it was in there somewhere. I wasn't about to pay $27 plus tax for a five-dollar foot long, chips and drinks not included. I *thought* I had a valid free Subway sandwich, eight magic stamps on my card, but it turns out it expired in March of 1991. After the chain got bought by the Saudi government, they switched to a new rewards system with no stamps, just an app you had to download and a byzantine points ladder that changed values based on the time of day and weather. Like I think you earned double points on Thursdays, but got double redemption of points on Tuesdays, or maybe it was the other way around? It probably never even gives out free sandwiches, and only harvested email addresses. I never got the right reward combinations, so I never got a free item. I wanted to light the store on fire, including that stupid woman in her stupid sweater and her stupid glasses on a chain making a stupid BMT sandwich and stupidly telling me it stood for Bread, Meat, Tomatoes. Stupid. It's technically not arson if it's a hate crime. BMT IS THE NAME OF A NEW YORK SUBWAY SYSTEM. BROOKLYN-MANHATTAN TRANSFER SYSTEM, MOTHERFUCKER. IT HAS EXISTED SINCE 1923.

Fuck this. Fuck Subway. Fuck everyone. I bolted, left the custom sandwich behind, let her deal with it. I could have paid cash, but that's not the point. Sometimes you have to make a stand. I saw this on the back of a No Fear sleeveless t-shirt once, so it must be right. Besides, I'm sure that woman ate 57 pounds of mistake orders a day. It's not like my no-sale personally killed starving kids in Africa. (That was their spokesman. Allegedly.) She was obviously a Christian; she wore a gigantic cross on her chest, like almost full scale. So forgive me.

The crap Chinese place next door guaranteed an extreme gastrointestinal malady that would rival a burst appendix on a ten-point pain scale, but there was no wait, so I went in and pointed at three random bowls of fried factory chicken with a slightly different coating of congealed Day-Glo sauce. The place had a generic Chinese-restaurant-sounding name, Golden Dragon or Lucky Phoenix or Diarrhea Star or whatever, but it was a mall franchise run by Iranian Islam extremists who had pictures of Ayatollah Khomeini on the wall, official portraits as well as candid snapshots the owner took at the leader's 1989 funeral, where over a sixth of the population of Iran came to Tehran, lining the streets in the scorching June heat. They also had a Khomeini noodles appetizer, basically just a re-labeled chow mein with goat meat in it. I don't think any of the typical anti-muslim circle-jerk gave them any flak, either because they didn't go to "ethnic" restaurants, or they didn't know how to read or even remember who Khomeini was, because that was like 50,000 news cycles ago. Don't expect any American to remember something happening 28 seasons of *Dancing With the Stars* ago.

I ate in silence at the counter/table, one of those stupid chest-high things with no chairs, designed to make people eat while standing for minimal loitering. A TV mounted to the ceiling droned on about how some asshole wanted to build a Forever 21 clothing store on the surface of the moon, and replace both the staff and the shoppers with robots so no humans would actually have to go there. It seemed like a stupid idea, but then I remembered how someone built a Prada store in the middle of the desert in Texas, like as a conceptual art piece. (Maybe not *in the middle of*. It was like a few miles from Marfa, Texas, which is where they shot the wedding scene in *Fandango*, and Larry Clark shot the movie *Marfa Girl*. I think Ben Lerner already covered this.)

The stomach attack started before I even finished the mystery chicken and its thick, syrupy orange sauce. It felt like a gall bladder explosion, but I couldn't remember which side of the abdomen was the gall bladder or the appendix, and then I started worrying that I might have that rare disorder where all of your internal organs are reversed. (*Situs inversus*. It's a real thing. One in ten thousand people. Enrique Iglesias and Catherine O'Hara both have it.) I tried to think of every x-ray and CT scan I'd ever had in my life while I prepared to shit my pants in the parking lot, tried to remember if I had any scans of my guts, where I could reference the orientation of the organs. I broke my arm one time, had a knee x-rayed, head CT for that sinus infection I was sure was an alien implant, dental checkups — no visceral organs imaged. Oh, I did have an ultrasound of my liver. I think that was the right side. Maybe they videotaped my colonoscopy, but that was so long ago, it was probably U-matic 3/4-inch tape.

Can't doctors just tap your abdomen and visualize where stuff is, or maybe use a stethoscope? I don't know. I didn't even have a primary care physician. I took exactly one health class as an undergrad and that was a Dimensions of Cancer class I ended up in because I wanted to fuck the instructor. I had to write a paper and because Frank Zappa died of prostate cancer, I did 50 pages on the 1988 *Guitar* double album and how the track titles, which have nothing to do with the actual tracks themselves, were a social allegory and were written by an unreliable narrator in the same way fictional neighbor Charles Kinbote wrote the commentary for fictional poet John Shade's *Pale Fire*, depicted in Vladimir Nabokov's novel of the same name. I think she didn't actually read it, and gave me a C.

North American Rescue makes something called a SPEAR - a Simplified Pneumothorax Emergency Air Release Device, a giant spike of a 10-gauge needle with a flexible catheter and a removable one-way valve. When someone gets a collapsed lung, a first responder can jab the thing into the chest between two ribs and relieve the pressure through the valve. I don't know if it's possible, but I thought about if I had one, I could jam it into my gut somehow and deflate whatever was going on in there. I'm absolutely sure I would put it in the wrong place and damage my liver or do something that would forever nullify my health insurance. Also, it's a prescription device, and I'm pretty sure the web site would not take a scan of my Doctor of Divinity card and allow me to buy anything.

I wandered down the street, clutching my gut, hoping I could just shit my pants and get it over with. A beaten and weathered Pepsi vending machine stood outside a Shop-Rite grocery store that had been torched for insurance money, but still looked semi-operational. After shoveling eighteen dollars of change into the machine, it spat out a plastic bottle of Sierra Mist. Warm, of course. I chugged it, hoping it would get rid of the internal pressure. I think I saw this in a Michael J. Fox movie where he was a rural doctor, or maybe went back in time and became a doctor? Did the doctor have epilepsy, or does he in real life? Did the epilepsy happen because of time travel? Or was it Parkinson's? They just wrote a report saying space travel — or extended zero-g time — can mess up your eyesight long-term. So who knows. We're all time travelers, moving one second into the future every second.

The corpse of the Shop-Rite sat across from a Costco, which I think was the first Costco ever built, although maybe they just said it was the first built, like how Ray Kroc said his Chicago McDonald's was the first location ever, when really, it was the first location *he* ever built, and he's a megalomaniacal dick. I had a flashback to a time when I bought a Black Sabbath-themed futon at that Costco. It came with a wooden frame, assembly required — lots of 4-mm hex bolts. I stupidly showed up with an old Ford Escort, thought it would be no problem hauling it home in that, and of course it was a major problem. I had to take everything out of the box, roll up the mattress like a huge joint, then fold down every seat and put all the pieces and the doobie/futon thing in the hatchback, sticking all the way up to the front windshield. I couldn't see out of the right side of the car at all, and it was pouring rain outside. But what the hell, one right turn, then get on the highway, drive home, and I'd make it, maybe. If not, I had insurance.

I also bought a large drum of dehydrated sour cream and onion soup on that trip, a chunky powder, like Cup-a-Soup, but the Kirkland brand, and like ten pounds in one cardboard tube, instead of the single-serving packet approach. Less waste, presumably. Save the earth. I knew this would not end well, dehydrated soup and a stomach aneurysm or whatever I had going on, but I bought it anyway, because I am a goddamn genius. It was the last of my money, and I expected to live off the can of dried soup for the rest of the month. I ended up selling a bunch of old death metal albums instead, eating McDonald's hamburgers and buying a sheath of bagels and a tub of fat-free cream cheese that was basically wall spackling, but it got me through until payday.

That was a long time ago. Anyway, the soda trick worked — I belched like a sailor, relieved the internal pressure. Pants unshat, I avoided a visit to urgent care and a speech about how I needed to diet and exercise. I would live to die another day. I went to Home Depot to look at the jackhammers and see if they had any of those explosive-charge nail guns like Snoop used on *The Wire*. They didn't.

PI IS TWO, GOD DAMN IT

I'm in a town in Arizona that has outlawed calculating the area of circles, and every viaduct and culvert is completely fucked. Any time they have a flash flood, almost all the infrastructure in the county is instantly destroyed by the deluge. Some random outback sheriff must have whipped people in a frenzy about Archimedes and Greek terrorists, passed a constitutional amendment to criminalize basic geometry. They already don't teach it in schools, so the only people who it affected were structural engineers in the state, who have all since died of alcoholism or scurvy.

I hadn't been in a Holiday Inn that still had a piano lounge and an indoor pool in maybe twenty-five years, but this place still looked like peak 1963 inside. Most of the Holiday Inns I've seen for the last few decades are generic prefab boxy micro-hotels that look like a typical Hyatt or Marriott or whatever, and maybe have a tray of bagels that are always 90% empty, and nothing else. This place was so old-school, they still let people smoke in the lounge. And the piano had an actual person playing and singing, albeit they were playing Billy Joel's "Piano Man" in an endless loop. Maybe it was a robot. Maybe this was a punishment for their sins. I don't know.

I sat at the bar, double-fisting cokes to stay awake, wishing I could drive my rental car straight into the Grand Canyon and never have to listen to this shit again. Can you catch air if you hit the edge of the GC, or have they put up some bollards or something to prevent that? I don't even know how far away the Grand Canyon is, except that it's far. You'd think Arizona, desert, one place, it's right on the edge of town, but I think it's five hours away. And probably not a straight shot, either. More like a winding two-lane bullshit run where you end up behind an RV going twenty below the limit for eight hours.

An unemployed firefighter with untreatable brain cancer and a plate in his head blocked my car in when I tried to cut across the hotel parking lot on the way to buy new bolt cutters because Werner Herzog told me to. He wore a Hawaiian shirt, looked like retired military or a burned-out security guard. He nursed a big fruity drink, with little fruit and a heavy pour, given the general color and viscosity of the liquid, and attempted to explain to me the history of the city's downfall since I last briefly crossed the region twenty years before, like I cared. I didn't want to start a conversation because I thought some terrorist group or religion had co-opted the Hawaiian shirt from the tech bros that usually wore them on a wild and crazy Friday, but I couldn't remember.

"Lindsey Buckingham's brother was an Olympic swimmer, you know," he said. "Allegedly won a silver at the '68 games in Mexico City. I say allegedly, because the common theory is that Stanley Kubrick helped the IOC completely fake the summer games on a sound stage not too far from here, right up the road at Davis-Monthan Air Force Base. Mexico had some kind of student revolt right before the games were supposed to be held, so they had to reshoot everything. Or maybe it was the Soviet invasion of Czechoslovakia? I don't know. I just had a buddy who snapped up a bunch of Super Panavision lenses and a Mitchell BFC 65mm camera for almost nothing from a rental house in Tucson. Primo stuff."

"Isn't that the games that had the controversy about the black power salute?"

"Exactly. Made-for-tv moment. It was even shot in full 4K with Dolby Atmos sound. And I'm sure Kubrick did something similar in *2001*, I just can't remember. Metal plate in my head, you know. Got shot in the head back in '83 by a crazy schizophrenic who thought he was bulletproof because he ate ten Hardee's hamburgers with cheese every day for a year. He tried proving this at the mall one Christmas at the Santa display and I was working as an elf helper, got hit by the ricochet. Luckily it was a cheap East German revolver, a .22 Short, Saturday Night Special. A good ten-pump pellet gun would have done worse. Still needed the plate though. Fucking doctors."

"Hey, do you know if that Safeway across the highway is still open? I need to get more Cokes and not at room service prices. The clerk at the front desk mentioned it but then had some kind of seizure and I didn't get a complete answer out of her."

"That grocery store went under overnight. No warning. Everyone who worked there showed up one day and the doors were bolted shut, everything inside moved in the dead of night. Same thing happened at the other Holiday Inn, the one north of town by the perpetual garbage fire," he said. "The damn British bought the place, jacked up the rates, ran it bankrupt. They locked the doors and left it empty for ten damn years. We could have turned it into affordable housing!"

I remember an urban exploration channel on YouTube where some dumb hipsters broke into that hotel years ago. This was the old Holidome setup with the indoor pool in the middle, all enclosed by a sixties-looking biosphere. Every surface inside was covered with a thick coat of stachybotrys chartarum, lethal black fungus. The explorers only got about fifteen minutes into their live broadcast before the mycotoxins completely destroyed them from the inside out. It would have been safer to walk straight into Chernobyl reactor 4 in 1986 naked and start licking the Elephant's Foot of radioactive black corium after dusting it with a fine powder of red dye and agent orange.

"Is that place still standing?" I wondered if the urban explorers' bodies were still sealed in the hotel tomb. Maybe I could fly a drone in there to look for their corpses, like James Cameron did with the Titanic. It's a bit morbid, but

I'm running out of ideas for hobbies, and I'm sure as fuck not going to start playing golf.

"Naw, they tore that thing down years ago. Said they were gonna build a Chick-fil-A but they put in this little mini mall, like a strip of six or eight stores, and then they didn't rent out a damn one. I think they had a vape store for a minute, but that's about it."

I wanted to find whatever kind of black mold I could inhale that would kill the part of my brain that controlled nostalgia. Just destroy everything but my short term memory. I don't even need that, honestly. I can write stuff down on my phone in the reminders app. I already pretty much have to do that anyway.

I wondered if the nachos were at all edible in a place like this, or if I was better off ordering something deep fried, like maybe chicken fingers, to make sure all the latent germs were killed. I asked a bus boy for his opinion on the matter and he told me they don't even cook the food there, don't have a kitchen. When people order stuff, he has to run next door to a Circle K, then take the food out of the to-go boxes and plate it. Maybe it gets nuked in the micro for 30 seconds if it's particularly bad, but maybe not. That didn't instill much confidence, but I ordered some roller grill mystery meat and a pretzel as big as my head anyway.

"...I thought about different things I could do with this much vacant land — maybe a fighting robot arena of some sort. Add some sexual component so people are more interested. Either there's really slutty announcers, or maybe you can pay extra and fuck the robots. But if people even vaguely thought that plan would be anti-Jesus in any way, kiss your ass goodbye. And everyone knows the only way to start a giant fighting robot league is to either involve devil worship or sodomy, so good luck with that."

An unrelated story about shitty pancakes and nuclear war

"Let's get us some fuckin' pannycakes!" Freddy kicked me in the back with his velcro Keds while I tried to sleep on the floor of the Satanic man-cave room in his mom's basement. Spending the night at Freddy's was always the worst possible scenario. Everything smelled like sweat, pepperoni pizza, and jizz, covered with the heavy odor of a bad Yankee Candle. It was bad enough he kept me up until three in the morning, babbling on with some insane theory about how every political assassination in the last 167 years was directly or indirectly related to autoerotic asphyxiation. I'd probably also end up paying for breakfast.

Aside from the smells and bizarro political commentary preventing any deep sleep, there were the noises. During the night, every seven minutes on the dot, a sump pump kicked on with a hundred and ten decibels of electronic buzzing and whirring like the gatling cannon on an anti-tank attack aircraft. Its shit-sucking impeller blades ran on an ancient analog clock circuit, a logic-less timer system triggering the power circuit exactly every 420 seconds, day and night. That always ended up happening roughly ten seconds after I blacked out. It was like sleeping on a plane while a seven-year-old body-slammed the back of your chair for the entire flight, except planes serve alcohol you can mass-consume to deaden the senses. And as a last resort, you could always pop open an emergency exit hatch and kill everyone onboard from rapid decompression. With luck, you'd get sucked out of the aircraft hull and fall 40,000 feet. But with my luck, I'd fall eye-first onto the edge of a razor-sharp manila folder balanced on the edge of a desk.

"Why are you so excited about breakfast?" I said. "It's only a few hours until lunch. Just fucking deal with it." I looked for my glasses, amongst the empty donut boxes, half-eaten Doritos bags, and pornographic glossy pictures of photoshopped airplane crashes, a long-standing fetish of his, and the reason he was permanently banned from every air museum in the tri-state area. (Freddy wasn't even allowed within 500 feet of those kiddie airplane rides in front of K-Marts and department stores that shake up and down when you put a quarter in them. And because his lifetime ban from Lane Bryant stores prevented him from going to any mall in the state, he could only shop at Big R Farm Supply, or the sad grocery store on the south side of town that exclusively took food stamps, so if you weren't on WIC, you had to buy some hot coupons from a dude in the parking lot.)

"If you don't eat breakfast, you gain weight," he said. "That's how sumo wrestlers bulk up. Ancient Chinese secret. They wake up before dawn, work out for a few hours on an empty stomach, eat five thousand calories of fish head stew, then take a long nap. Fucks up your metabolism, slows it down so you can practically gain weight in minutes. True story — David Lee Roth explained it once on the Joe Rogan podcast."

"David Lee Roth let Eddie Van Halen play keyboards once. What the fuck does he know about nutrition? I saw a picture of him recently and he looks like the fucking crypt keeper. Maybe if it was a breakfast of brown M&M's and cocaine, he would know full details on it. Fuck you and your pancakes, and the bacon memes you're going to start up with in ten seconds. Fuck bacon and fuck Ron Swanson. This isn't 2013 anymore, motherfucker. Stop singing 'Friday, Friday' and get your fucking act together. I'm going back to bed. Your mother's a whore."

Freddy's lack of timeliness about memetic culture annoyed me to the point of violence. We're talking about a guy who still watched South Park, and actually found "Got Milk?" parodies funny. He quoted *Family Guy* constantly, and I knew it was only a matter of time before he bought some of those "Keep Calm and _____" shirts, or leaned hard into the Budweiser "wazzup" thing.

He turned on a klieg light in the corner, something he used when precision-assembling model airplanes to light on fire and jerk off to. It blinded me instantly, involuntarily sending me into a tirade of screaming obscenities and quotes from vampire movies that I only remembered because various 90s death metal bands sampled them. "Okay, I'm fucking awake. Do I get a shower first, or do I have to bring the stench of the dead to the pancake place?"

"Fuck showers. We need to get a table before the fucking churches empty out and the bootleg Denny's is full of Jesus freaks. I don't know what god has to do with high-fat food, but that Venn diagram is a fucking circle. You've got five minutes to take a piss and a whore's bath, dump some of that Drakkar on, and let's get the fuck out of here. You drive."

* * *

The place was called Danny's, and it was a wholesale ripoff of the national chain of a similar name, in the borderline humorous fashion of bootleg Chinese toys for Robert Cop and Star Track. It had the same red-on-yellow signage, but was inside a former first-generation Taco Bob, which meant it only seated a dozen people in tiny two-up brown plastic booths, and you ordered at a counter instead of table service. It sat next to a Big O Tire shop that did swift business because some genius working there dumped a bag of roofing nails on the four-lane out front every day. They also cut catalytic converters out of tuned import cars and put those farty-sounding mufflers on riced-out Hondas for dudes in their early twenties who worked as dishwashers because they couldn't get into college and couldn't pass the piss test for the Army.

I glanced at a grease-soaked menu, and tried to determine which combo offered the correct ratio of meats to eggs. These places always liked to fuck you over, and go heavy on the bread or potatoes, whatever was cheapest. Four eggs, eight pieces of bacon, one pancake, one side of toast. Nothing else. Why can't anyone get that right? "Sumo diet or not, I don't think you're losing any weight if you order an entire pound of bacon and sixteen pancakes."

"Doctors hate this one simple trick! The bacon grease makes my heart run more efficiently. It's just like putting synthetic oil in your car. My uncle sold AmsOil for years, until he went to federal prison for tax evasion. Fuck the FDA and their stupid healthy diets."

"Synthetic oil doesn't add performance to your engine. It just resists wear, and costs more."

"Then I'll live forever. My heart flaps and valves and whatever else the fuck is going on in there will never wear out. Paying the extra two dollars per side of bacon is a small price to pay for immortality. Plus it's tasty. Got bacon?"

I ordered the Grand Slap, the main breakfast, which if it was a direct copy of a Grand Slam, would have been two eggs, two pancakes, two pieces of bacon, and two sausages. But Danny's did a gimmick where they doubled everything, so you got four eggs, four pancakes, etc. They made this economically feasible by using the lowest-quality ingredients, like powdered eggs, and rubbery, frozen grade-D mystery meat. Everyone in town loved it, though, not because of quality, but because of quantity. If there was a business here where they made you dig your own grave and shot you in the head, and they ran a two-for-one sale and gave away a free Garth Brooks tape to the first thousand customers, they would have people camping in line for days to get in on the deal.

We were crammed into one of the small booths, no room for coats or elbows or anything else. After an hour of impatience, our bearded-lady waitress brought out two trays filled with lard and carbohydrates. The sticky plastic trays took up 116% of the table's surface area, and were obviously stolen from an Arby's. I sawed at one of my sausages with a blunt butter knife, and it was like chopping a granite statue in half with a plastic spatula.

"You fell asleep before I finished my explanation of the assassination thing last night," he said, while shoveling bacon into his fat maw. "I didn't even tell you my theory on how Ron Paul could really win this time. It's fucking genius. Can you flag down this waitress and ask to borrow her pen? I'll draw it out on the back of this placemat." He picked up his paper placemat, and it was soaked in grease like it had a bottle of Wesson oil upended on it. "Actually, ask her for a new placemat, too."

"I barely slept, so I'm sure most of your political science lecture made it into my head by osmosis."

"Yeah, that's what Nate fuckin' Silver said, too. And look what happened to that dude. I think he's dealing blackjack on an Indian reservation in Oklahoma now." He stuffed an entire sausage in his mouth, barely started chewing, and spit pieces of half-masticated pork as he lectured me. "You ever been to Oklahoma? I had a cousin who lived there, used to fly C-5 Galaxy jets in the Army," Freddy said. "The ones with the nose that swings up so they can drive in tanks, you know what I mean? Jam a GI Joe tank right up that thing's windpipe, no problemo. It could carry like a dozen and a half Apache helicopters in its bowels, and it had machine guns on top of it, and he was an operator and used to fly it on special forces missions in a secret war he can't even legally talk about. But he got busted sucking dick for coke at this biker bar right off base. He also pissed hot on a drug test, and kept failing his physical fitness test because he ate at the base Taco Bob five times a day, so they kicked him to the curb. No hope in dope. He got disability though — not through the service, but the social security kind. Faked a back injury in a Teledyne weapons factory parking lot, got a good lawyer who said it was in the federal jurisdiction or something, so he did okay. No pain pills anymore, but he gets a massage at this rub-and-tug every month, fully paid for by the government. He mostly plays PlayStation all day now. Smokes a ton of dope, too. He was in the top thousand on the *Call of Duty* leaderboard at one point. Got a free t-shirt or some shit."

I wasn't listening — I was trying to calculate the most I could buy from Taco Bob for $863, like what would be the largest amount of food possible, and if it would all fit in my car. There's some tricky math involved, and you need to start by deciding what constitutes "most" — total calories, total weight, maximum volume, biggest shit taken after eating it, etc. Like you could probably max out calories by ordering a single taco and 862 sides of guacamole, but I wouldn't want to eat it. I thought the best strategy would involve ordering all tacos, which is boring, but the twelve-packs would be economical in bulk. 725 tacos at 170 calories each, which is a pretty straightforward calculation. But a Dollar Cravings Menu Beefy Fritos Burrito is going to be 430 calories and only a dollar each, so that might be the ticket there... Does my phone still have a calculator app, or did they make that an optional purchase, too?

"...And then his neighbor used to pay my girlfriend to watch us fuck. I wasn't that into it at first, but she saved up the money and got a Super Nintendo. It had a pretty good *Tetris*, from what I remember, and a decent *Star Wars* platform game, I think for *Empire Strikes Back*. I played a lot of *SimCity* on that bitch. Did you know the Nintendo version of *SimCity* replaced the Godzilla attack with a Bowser attack?"

"Wait, this dude would pay to watch you to fuck your girlfriend? I didn't even know you had a girlfriend."

"I was dating this girl back then who worked at a Toll House cookie factory. She wasn't elf-sized or anything, though. And she never got free cookies, either — they were really good about destroying any mistake batches, so people wouldn't get poisoned. Yeah. I think that neighbor wanted to join in — he was a pretty creepy little fucker. Really into women's feet. I think he said his mom used to give him enemas as a kid. He was also into Mötley Crüe, Poison, all those butt-rock arena metal bands. Always quoted their songs when he was watching us. You ever try fucking out someone while a weird little dude was singing 'Nothin' but a good time?' Christ. Hey, have you ever put cayenne pepper on mango before?"

"What the fuck are you talking about? Like as a sex thing?"

"No, just in general. I think I saw it on *Larry King Live* once. I don't remember who was on there talking about it. Prince Charles, I think. You buy mango from those Mexican dudes on the side of the road in LA, and they sprinkle hot pepper on it. I don't know why it works, but it works. That's what I think about when a chick bulletproofs her car. God damn! I don't know why I like it, but I like it."

I couldn't remember ever knowing a woman with a bulletproof car, although I did know a morbidly obese librarian who drank six cups of bulletproof coffee every morning, the stuff made with a stick of butter in it. She died of a heart attack, and nobody could yell for help, because it was in a library, and you're supposed to keep quiet. Lol.

We finished eating, and then Freddy did the where's-my-wallet thing, and I ended up paying for both of us, of course.

* * *

By the time we got back to Freddy's, his stepdad had burned down the house trying to light sugar cubes on fire, and Freddy went spontaneously blind. We went to urgent care and he got diagnosed with Anton–Babinski syndrome, which is a rare symptom of brain damage to the occipital lobe in which a person has complete visual blindness but insist they can still see. I never met the Toll House chick he was purportedly dating. It didn't matter because three days later, there was a nuclear war and the entire world died. The end.

From the 2023 Breyerlin Baseline Cognitive Performance Survey (BBCPS)

7) You are on a prison bus. The woman chained to you goes into labor and has a baby. The child is born with a full beard and thick pubic hair. The bus stops in a Burger Chef parking lot, a franchise that has been dead since 1982. The bus driver is David Letterman. Do you:

A) Go to the Burger Chef and see if they have the Super Shef burger?

B) Shave the child?

C) Sing the Aerosmith song "Sweet Emotion"?

D) Tell David Letterman about a really bad reuben sandwich you ate in Muncie, Indiana in 1987?

12) Business owners who have commercial premises often tend to have residential property as part of their portfolio.

A) True

B) False

C) Only if they hunt human beings from a helicopter in Alaska

D) Cannot tell

18) You're friends with a boy who your mom used to babysit. He has renounced his American citizenship, moved to Afghanistan, joined Al Qaeda, and the FBI has a $500,000 award for his capture for several counts of treason. He calls you at work from a stolen cell phone and offers to pay you to bring a pallet of Stinger missiles to China, where his operatives will smuggle them across the Kashmir trail to him. Do you:

A) Report your mother to the IRS for operating an unlicensed day care?

B) Hang up the phone, because taking personal phone calls is against company policy?

C) Advise your friend that Raytheon now offers a service-extension upgrade to the Stinger that replaces the integral battery and increases accuracy and range of the infrared lock-on guidance, and he should contact a Raytheon service representative for a quote?

D) Change your phone number before you start getting calls from reporters?

22) A soup kitchen makes 1200 gallons of soup per week, at $4.00 per quart. If the cost per quart rises to $4.50 because the kitchen was caught using human blood in their soup

base and have to switch to cow blood, how much more will the kitchen have to pay for soup per week?

A) $30

B) $40

C) $45

D) It doesn't matter because soup is bullshit.

79) You are debugging microcode for the Western Digital Center 65C02 microprocessor on an Apple IIc. Your code crashes when performing ANC #i ($0B ii). Why?

A) Satan.

B) This is a known issue with the ArchUsr64/6502_emulator debugger. Try using Sakrac/Step6502.

C) This is an unimplemented opcode in the 6502, but it's implemented in the 65C02, causing non-portable code.

D) Time is not real.

Intestinal Vestibule

The cake men of doom brought their wrath to the river-front, flooding the houses with liquid fudge and psychosis. I saw a PTA mom run down the road, skin on fire, her hair covered with raspberry preserves, screaming at her lawn sprinklers about the failure of Russian typewriters. I tried to record her speech on my flip-phone's message recorder, so I could maybe sample it later for a post-industrial one-man noise band, but the cheap Samsung didn't use a standard file format, and when I later bought the six different adapter cables to plug the phone into my computer, Windows kept trying to open the sounds in WordPerfect.

I covered the walls with tractor-feed paper, the lime green and off-white stripes forming a protective layer from the blood of demonic possession and vomit of the living. It also kept the model glue off the walls so maybe I'd get back 0.01% of my deposit back when I moved out. At my *Barney Miller* card table, the primo yard sale score of a lifetime, I painstakingly assembled a model of Penn Station built out of organ meats I found in a dumpster behind the IGA. None of it made sense, but I hoped it would, eventually. The heavy glue I used to laminate and attach the offal had fumes that teleported me into the 17th dimension of grog, and I fought it as long as I could, trying to get the intestinal vestibule completed.

That card table was pure luck, given it was right before Hal Linden started a one-man pornogrind noise band that used his birth name, The Lipshitz, and one of his tracks got sampled by Taylor Swift, and now all *Barney Miller* merch is unobtanium. But I worked with a guy who had a section of Dwight Eisenhower's bypassed colon, preserved in a glass Ball jar commemorating the 25th anniversary of the first issue of *Hustler* magazine. Went to his house one night to look at it, and didn't have the heart to tell him it was a replica, not the real deal.

A stranger appeared in my half-asleep dream state, dressed in the uniform of a CalTrans toll booth operator, wearing a throwback San Diego Padres hat. He was handcuffed to a man who looked like a Hispanic Elvis two days before he left this world trying to pinch a loaf on his Graceland throne: greasy sideburns, a sequined jumpsuit hiding his rolls of fat, and even a glitter-covered cape. I could tell this dude spent a lot of his time throwing fake karate chops in the air and eating fried peanut butter sandwiches.

It made me think of black hair dye, a coke machine with glass bottles, and an Amiga video game where you hit aliens in the junk with a sledgehammer, and a synthesized voice said "groovy!" over and over. I didn't know the order or relevance of the items, just that they happened. Somewhere, under the sink, was a waterproof space pen and a pad of plastic paper, something to capture the thoughts, but before I could find it, everything vanished from my brain, and I was left holding my dick in the darkness, completely blank inside.

Corporate Sanitation of Cadaveric Beef Through Mechanical Violence

Some dude in jorts and boat shoes with white socks ran through the housewares section of the Zayres department store with a chainsaw, yelling about Commodore Amiga memory upgrade prices. The Guy ignored him, just wanting to buy or steal a comforter with a groovy Nineties color scheme, lots of hot pink and teal, maybe something synthetic. His current bedding had a vintage *Empire Strikes Back* print on it, and this was years before the whole nerd-equals-cool thing, so it wasn't working out well with the ladies. He can't believe how overwhelming the smell of unburned gas/oil mix from the saw is within the concealed space. He must have inhaled an endless amount of that petroleum vapor when he was a kid mowing lawns, but now it's so overpowering, he'd have the smell of Stihl MotoMix stuck in his nostrils for the rest of the day.

[Editor here. I think that Jedi *perfectly summed up the end of childhood for me. I spent my formative years worshipping the first two films; they were like an impenetrable theme through the years from 1977 to 1983, from Kindergarten up to the sixth grade. Then,*

when I was twelve, I got this total let-down of an end of a trilogy. Darth Vader is killed, and the big reveal when they pull his mask off is that this evil badass James Earl Jones dude is really a pale, fat, bald-headed guy with a harmonica-looking thing jammed in his mouth. He looked like my fat Uncle Barry before he got sent to the can for tax evasion. Also don't forget that Ewok bullshit. So Vader is a let-down, they kill off Boba Fett, they basically repeat half of the first film by destroying another Death Star, and a few months later, my parents have filed for divorce and I have found out adults are stupid and fallible, all of my little plastic figurines are useless, and my next long hobby is the next half-century of wondering why I can't get laid.]

Hours later, The Guy is talking to an octogenarian man with lightning bolts shaved into the sides of his head, and a sweet mullet going on in the pack. He's sucking down a filterless camel while wearing an oxygen tank, and The Guy is wondering when it will explode. They're in front of an auto glass place on Main that has to be a front for drugs, because he's never seen them replace a windshield, ever. They don't even have any windshields from modern cars on display, just old non-safety glass from Studebakers and Dusenbergs.

"There used to be a candlemaker on this street," said the old man. "Ran a rub-and-tug place at night. You could get jerked off with wax for ten bucks on Tuesday and Thursday nights. They ended up shutting it down because of some damn law about chandlers washing their hands when they handle scented wax. The owner murder-suicided, and a year

later, this Chinese family bought the dump at probate auction, opened up a crap Chop Suey joint. Damn shame.
Aside from the stress relief service, they used to sell scented
potpourri on the cheap. I must have dumped thousands of
dollars there on nag champa and hand jobs over the years.
All we get in return is MSG and the shits."

"Kroger's got a candle section. Not as good as Bath and
Body, but it's pretty cheap and you can pick up a steak or
some sausage on the same trip."

"Fuck Kroger's. Fuck their candles and fuck their meat
counter. Had a cousin that started buying a quarter-share of
a cow every winter, butcher it in his garage with a hedge
trimmer. Tasty meat, too. It's risky business though, keeping
a chest freezer of meat going all year. So many goddamn
power outages in this town, you're rolling the dice on ending
up with a thousand dollars of rotting flesh at some point."

"That's not a big deal, I listen to a lot of gore-grind metal. Owning every Carcass album has sort of prepared me for
a garage full of decomposing meat. Plus I eat pretty fast. I
could probably clear a freezer of beef in under a month."

"Yeah, but the damn power goes out every other week
here in the winter. I don't know if the linemen are off sniff-
ing glue, or it's from every asshole who can't drive at the first
sign of ice, crashing into telephone poles. They're all drunk
too, or high on the weed. Why are we even using power

lines, anyway? Can't they just shoot the power across the air? I thought Tesla had this shit invented a hundred years ago."

"Nikola Tesla was assassinated by the FBI," The Guy said. "Nobody ever saw his body. They shipped an urn full of incinerated cat shit and food scraps to Belgrade and stashed all of his research in a secret government warehouse in West Virginia. And nobody talks about this, but Tesla was directly responsible for the invention of anime. If he would have survived World War II, they would have brought him to Nuremberg and executed him for war crimes."

"Well, I don't get into that government political shit," he said. "Had a neighbor who ended up in the can for ten years because he tried to kill a city council guy by putting coal dust in his gas furnace. He wanted to build a fence across his front yard so he could grow weed legally, and something about the easement and the utilities company. Red tape bullshit. I never followed his logic, but I learned a lesson about what you should tell others."

Head Like a Hole

I'm watching a twelve-part Ken Burns documentary on Shredded Wheat cereal. I have no interest in Shredded Wheat; I don't eat cereal, and it's one of the shittiest cereals made. Cheerios is probably second-worst, and Shredded Wheat is at least 78 times worse. It's basically wood pulp that's been engineered to scratch open your mouth. Regardless, I can't stop watching. I'm at part four or five, where he's covering the Nabisco Shredded Wheat/Quaker Shredded Wheat schism. The latter was created by the inventor's son thirty years later. I don't remember why; I think he covers it in the next episode; this one is mostly a montage of pan-and-scan on a still photo of a wheat mill at Niagara Falls. The show is good background music, I guess, provided it doesn't make me have a psychotic break.

Seven stories below, a man walked in a circle in the middle of the intersection of Seventh and James, yelling about Pearl Jam or intersecting splines or something involving a government rutabaga. (It was hard to hear over traffic, plus I honestly do not give a fuck.) James is a major arterial road, and on a main bus route. Seventh is where the first (or maybe second) exit of I-90 dumps out after crossing the lake and intersecting with I-5. As far as this dude potentially getting slammed by a bus, it was a matter of when, not if. I considered calling 911, but the apartment building recently switched to some Microsoft-based VoIP solution, and 911 never worked, or cost extra. Maybe I had to upgrade to a Windows landline or dial 1-900-911, I don't know.

I found it easier to mute the Ken Burns thing and turn on the stereo, but Seattle's a bad town for terrestrial radio. Everyone seems to say Seattle is great for radio, maybe because of Nirvana or Louie Louie, but I think the hills ruin it. I mean, now radio is just an app or channel online, or maybe you go to a web site and click on a widget. (Or you probably have to pay Comcast another twenty bucks to listen to it.) But back when you needed line-of-sight with an antenna, it was a problem. (Wait, is FM radio line-of-sight? I know the radio in a cell phone isn't, but that's because $1/r\,4$ propagation over the rooftop landscape bounces signals, and there are cell towers everywhere now. I remember a coworker telling me her phone always died in Battery Park because the World Trade Center interfered with the satellite transmission, and I had to mansplain that cell phones don't talk to satellites, they go to line-of-sight towers, and those were probably blocked. And then a year later, the WTC got blown up, and nobody in lower Manhattan had good cell service, and I think that coworker got a job with the CIA interrogating prisoners, and... what was I talking about?)

An hour later, I'm on the roof of the building eating microwaved hot dogs and watching a guy on a rampage who said he worked at Three Mile Island with Trent Reznor's cousin and can prove that Nine Inch Nails somehow caused Chernobyl. He's yelling at the cops seven stories below about how he's got charts and graphs, but they're all in Corel Draw, so they need to find him a DOS computer. I can't tell if this is the same guy who was on the street before, or a different one. He would have needed a key to get up there, but maybe someone buzzed him in. He was wearing a Domino's Pizza uniform, but I think it was just ironically or something.

The hot dogs were mostly a placeholder for real food, which I'd have to get shortly. I figured if I microwaved them, they would split open and get all disgusting, and I'd throw them out and go get some real food, but that didn't happen lol.

* * *

Fell into a deep depression over an ex who simultaneously doesn't even remember me but thinks I'm the worst thing that ever happened in her life. Not sure how that works, but I know I've wasted my entire day in a despair pit, wallowing in it something heavy. There's no easy way out of this situation, although I thought I could make it worse by day-drinking at a Showbiz Pizza and threatening people at the Tetris Plus machine, telling them I could kick their ass in the puzzle mode of the 1996 sequel. (Don't ask how I found a ShowBiz Pizza that was still operational. I thought they all got turned into Chuck E. Cheese or abandoned, but there was still one left. Maybe that's an indicator of the shittiness of my small town, I don't know.)

Walking home from the edge of town. I figure a 25-mile death march will take my mind off of things. Nothing like a foot or two full of blisters to clear the head. They built three Hardees locations out by auto mall road, right next to each other. The trick is to go to the one in the middle, because the drive throughs on the end ones are going to be more backed up. I thought through the possibility of a complex load-balancing system to evenly route cars to each building, something like the equivalent of the Nginx web server, but with a series of ramps and railroad turntables instead of HTTP traffic. Then I remembered the place sold four-dollar grease bombs with almost no profit margin, and they could barely pay their staff minimum wage. I was overthinking things. I went home, jerked off twice, and ate an entire Papa John's pizza (including that pepper and the container of garlic butter) in twelve bites. I still felt depressed.

* * *

Procedural trauma nightmares, nonstop terror: forever trying to get a formula in a spreadsheet to work without destroying the entire time-space continuum, hours clicking an interface that's unclickable in the dream realm, and then the cold sweat fear after waking up, thinking you've gotta get this goddamn Excel to work before your boss comes back from Manchuria with a truck full of severed heads and a Lucy Lawless RealDoll. Tell yourself over and over it isn't real, while you stumble to the bathroom for more sleeping pills, Benadryl, and painkillers.

The Ambien warning label is now required to have verbiage saying that in some rare cases, you may fly an AH-64D Apache Longbow attack helicopter and fire AGR-20A Advanced Precision Kill Weapon System precision-guided munitions at ground targets in your sleep, and you should talk to your doctor immediately if this happens. Wonder what lawsuit caused them to have to do that. The rockets themselves are getting a warning label, too. Luckily nobody knows how to read anymore. Instead of maintenance manuals, the new B-21 stealth bomber is getting a TikTok channel.

In 2019, some old geezer in Taiwan got killed when he tried to cut apart the warhead of a misfired AGR-20A Advanced Precision Kill Weapon System rocket with an electric saw. A fisherman caught the warhead in a net, thought it was a generic piece of metal tube, and dragged it ashore to sell it to a scrapper. The scrapper banged on it with a hammer for hours before taking the saw to it. Instant Darwin award. Lesson of the day: don't Sawz-all a ten-pound chunk of high explosives. Stick to aluminum cans and stolen copper wiring.

Instead of suffering in the conversations-from-eight-years-ago-replayed purgatory as I stared at the ceiling, racked with insomnia, I took the advice of some dumb web search and started excavating a large trench in my back yard in the middle of the night. Digging up graves at night helped Ed Gein sleep way before they invented Sonata. I wasn't sure what I was digging in my back yard, though. No graves there, but maybe there was some lost jewelry. How much does a good metal detector cost? I'm sure there's a reddit I can waste too much time on, shopping for more garbage I don't need. I'm not that far into my midlife crisis yet. Wake me up when we get to the Corvette purchase.

Searching for arrowheads used to be a big thing when I was a kid. Is that still a thing, or is it illegal now? Had a crazy uncle Harold who always went on about how you could sell them for a hundred bucks each, back when a hundred dollars would buy you a functional used car, rather than a single bag of groceries. I never believed him, partly because I spent endless hours looking for arrowheads and found nothing, but partly because he also talked about how he spent all this time in the Marines killing Vietcong in the jungle, and I knew for a fact he'd almost never been more than ten miles out of town, except one time he drove to Chicago for Disco Demolition Night at Comiskey Park, where he got a flaming shard of vinyl from a Bee Gees record rammed into his skull. The injury required emergency surgery and the insertion of a steel plate in his head, which is why he could never eat ice cream anymore. The plate caused a traumatic brain freeze and he would shit his pants and think he was back in the Vietnam he never went to in the first place every time he had ice cream.

Why can't they invent a Drumstick ice cream sundae but instead of all the ice cream at the top and just the very bottom point of the ice cream cone has got solid chocolate in it, make like an entire pound of the solid chocolate part? I honestly don't care about the ice cream, and will buy an entire box and throw out 90% of each cone and just eat the tail parts. Maybe there's some materials science/production issue, but they're shooting rockets to Mars every other week, they can get this sorted out.

Skippy: Unfinity

Skippy went to rehab for being addicted to *Magic: The Gathering* cards. It led to a series of chronic jaywalking tickets, and a judge said either he could join the Coast Guard and get sent to the war in Barbados or go to a lockdown rehab where they'd fill him with Cool Ranch lithium and positive affirmations. They forced him to drill holes through all of his cards while a priest read an exorcism book and screamed "THE POWER OF CHRIST COMPELS YOU" over and over. When he got out of the joint, he had to spend 200 hours reading to blind people, and ended up catching herpes. Insurance won't cover Valtrex if you get it from court-ordered therapy.

A pharmacy rep named Brooke chatted up the receptionist while Skip sat in the day room next to the lobby, completely cooked on a smooth blend of Thorazine, Vistaril, and Zofran. She talked about bank robberies, Mexican restaurants, and a dentist who went to prison for fake billing Medicare patients with a Stripe credit card machine he got from his nephew. Her voice both captivated and annoyed everyone. It was obvious she had 500cc breast implants. She started talking about how she wanted to fuck a dentist. "It's a good business to lock down. You have to be a dentist to own a dental clinic in this state. No speculators or absentee landlords possible."

Brooke drove a 2024 Mercedes W465 G-Wagon with all options, including the 4.0 L M177 V8 twin-turbo and bulletproof military glass. She got it painted pink, and had custom license plates that say DRUGDLR. She'd end up wrapping it around a tree after taking 14 Klonopin and heading out in a tornado. Her gigantic fat breast implants prevented a fatal thoracic injury, but she had to get them redone in Tijuana after the accident, and they never looked right again.

* * *

Timothy McVeigh's brother was selling time shares in the parking lot of a Filipino grocery store way the hell south of the Vegas Strip, contracts for Vegas hotels that haven't existed for decades. "I can get you in the Sands, one week a year for only a hundred bucks a month. Loose slots. Free continental breakfast from six to eight AM, five days a week!" Didn't they implode the Sands back in the Nineties? Maybe he's somehow honoring his brother's work? This was next to that townie casino where you could cash your paycheck, get a free pull on a rigged slot machine, then eat a live monkey's brain for $40. They got shut down, but not for animal cruelty; Arby's owned the *Faces of Death* franchise now and thought the monkey brain thing was copyright infringement and shut it the fuck down.

Dysentery was big that year, everyone walking around town with a bucket full of feces, blood clots, and cheese. Disease was the new BetaMax, the new Netflix, an endless stream of content for the masses. Need a germ, take a germ; have a germ, leave a germ. I'm not exactly a germaphobe, like a Howard Hughes, tissue boxes on feet, burn all clothes if someone in the building is sick germaphobe. Purell was mandatory. People carried bottles of hand sanitizer like a desert journeyman carried water.

Skippy went to Florida while on a furlough because someone in the joint told him there's a secret members-only VIP sex dungeon under Busch Gardens in Tampa. He heard there's a hidden door somewhere near the exit of the Kumba roller coaster, but he couldn't find it. He also tried to find Ace's Records, the record store that was the epicenter of Death Metal back in the early 90s. When he drove out to 1518 E Fowler Ave it was a Mexican barber shop and nail salon.

* * *

Skippy got out when his parents' HMO stopped paying and the clinic turfed him. He ended up in Seattle, because he became addicted to coffee, and everyone he knew in the Midwest who says "expresso" instead of "espresso" told him to move to the Pacific Northwest for the best joe. He didn't realize you can get the same coffee pretty much anywhere now. He did not move to Seattle because of Wizards of the Coast; he didn't realize the creator of his former addiction was headquartered a few miles from his apartment. He seldom left his apartment, anyway.

One day he went to a Chinese restaurant in the U-district called Hunan Centipede. He looked it up online and ironically, it was owned by a day-trader who doesn't have a stomach and never ate solid food. Other than the catchy name, the movie had nothing to do with the business. Their sweet and sour chicken was decent: good fry on the meat, and a respectable pineapple to chicken ratio, with only enough bell peppers to make it official and in no way healthy. If you liked spicy food at all, you were screwed. Their Szechuan chicken tasted like the sauce was made from Hunt's ketchup. It had no chiles in it and was about a two on the Scoville scale. No fortune cookies, either.

Infinite McDonald's

I'm asleep in the dining room of a Church's Chicken, and my face is stuck to the table. The booth's horizontal eating surface is a high-sheen fake wood that's sticky like flypaper, and when I wake up, it takes significant effort to pry my cheek from it. At first, there's an immense fear that I will pull loose the skin from my face and end up in a burn center for skin transplants, and I'll spend the rest of my life explaining that no, I didn't get in a car accident or fall asleep freebasing; I just blacked out at a shitty chicken restaurant.

The nightmare during the food coma: Infinite McDonald's. The company's current year-over-year revenue growth is largely flat, maybe 4-5% per year in the last decade. But what if their revenue growth was exponential and continued that way every year until the company approached infinite size? Because McDonald's is incorporated in Delaware but operates company-owned stores and collects franchise revenue from stores outside the United States, it must follow Generally Accepted Accounting Principles published by the Financial Accounting Standards Board in the United States, but also has significant income in regions following the International Financial Reporting Standards set by the International Accounting Standards Board. (FY2023 had GAAP net income of $8.468B vs. non-GAAP of $8.742B.)

This affects accounting for inventory, development costs, write-downs, and fixed-asset depreciation. (Example: PP&E assets under GAAP are recorded at historical cost and depreciated; under IFRS fixed assets can be revalued to FMV over time.) If McDonald's was infinite, IFRS and GAAP would be infinite but a reconciliation for non-GAAP gains, charges, and tax settlement would still be used to calculate non-GAAP net income and reconcile diluted earnings per common share. This would likely adversely affect pre-tax charges for growth strategy, even though at an infinite size it would still continue to grow and require programs like work modernization and software change charge-downs.

I suddenly realized I had tooth whitening trays in my mouth and was about to choke on the peroxide paste accumulation. This was 247% peroxide gel I bought at a Chinese drop-ship company that later got shut down for selling human corpses to those Body Worlds museum exhibits. No idea how it was more than 100%, but I drink so much soda, I have to do something. I desperately needed to rinse out my mouth and maybe brush my teeth a bit to remove the whitening solution, but that definitely wouldn't happen in a Church's Chicken bathroom.

* * *

I found a Coke machine outside that sold overpriced water. Warm, of course. Walked through an empty industrial park, swishing, spitting out the whitening crud, irrigating my mouth 167 times. This wasn't the kind of industrial park you'd think of if I said "gritty manufacturing complex" — it was more like a Silicon Valley commercial suburb, with plain white buildings set back from the street by a hundred yards, built in the early eighties when chips were manufactured in the US. They probably all sat empty, taken over by black mold. It was a Saturday afternoon, so the entire neighborhood was eerily silent.

Stumbled on a plaque in the middle of nowhere, just up from the sidewalk. It said that on that spot in 1964, a cargo jet crashed, raining a debris trail of over a million pounds of sea monkey eggs across the neighborhood. Luckily, as anyone who ever got Sea Monkeys as a kid, none of them lived past like a week, so there wasn't like a wild colony of feral Sea Monkeys that would have to be remediated by the Army Corps of Engineers, just a horrible smell of dead seafood that persisted for decades.

Got out my phone to search if sea monkey is a branded term, and of course the sign is wrong. Sea-Monkeys® is an active registered trademark of The Original Sea Monkeys Partnership, Reg. No. 0747689 with the U.S. Patent and Trademark Office (USPTO). So would "sea monkey eggs" or "Sea-Monkeys® eggs" be correct usage? Three clicks into the rabbit hole, I find that Harold von Braunhut, the inventor of the aforementioned eggs and X-Ray Specs, was a notorious white supremacist, buying firearms for the Klan and frequently attending the national Aryan Nations annual conference. Despite being ethnically Jewish, he ran the National

Anti-Zionist Institute from the same PO box as his Sea-Monkeys business. I should probably block Wikipedia at the router level on every internet-connected device I own and get back like a decade of my life.

My car was two miles away, and I was completely out of energy, didn't want to walk any more, but I had no choice. I hate when I do this, but there's probably a business opportunity here, because it forced me to exercise. Maybe I could rent a van, paint a sick mural of a wizard on the side, come up with a bulletproof business pitch, then drive people to the wilderness and dump them off ten miles from civilization. I mean, there are people who have made millions forcing gym bros to basically pay to do the Army boot camp without the guns or the haircuts. Maybe this can be the next big thing. Infinite growth potential.

Statue of Limitations

This story begins with a man, a dream, and a statue. Or maybe it's a man, a garbage fire, and an unfortunate problem.

The dream: I'm in a mall. Always in a mall, on the edge of a town with a secret. Unrelated, but there's a secret floor underneath the shopping center — everything has an underground level below the street, from a century before. The city burned down, some folklore about a bull kicking over a lantern, and they rebuilt anew on top of the ruins. Some stores have a hidden passage to access the carbon-scorched brick tunnels underground, which are completely sealed off from the world. It's a good place to fuck an assistant manager of a GNC or Walden Books, if that's your deal.

I sit underneath a vacant bank, eating chicken tenders from a plastic bus tray, reading a Buck Rodgers paperback anthology that had the comic strips in the wrong order. I think they used AI to put it together, but why blame AI when it just sucks in the first place. The comics make no sense, but I only scanned them out of boredom. I always need to be reading and never have anything to read. Thought about tattooing Moby-Dick on my arms in microscopic print, but then I remembered Melville wrote that giant tome in only 18 months, and I've been screwing with this 30,000-word disaster for years now and I'm making zero progress, so why remind myself daily for the rest of my life.

The randomness of the comic strips also makes the reading seem like a dream, drifting from plot to plot with no structure, no device to get from place to place. I think about this within the dream, but I don't think that my own random movement within the dream is anything out of the ordinary, and don't consciously think that I was in a dream. But the concept of a dream within a dream makes me think about launching subprocesses from processes in a multitasking operating system, and it makes me wonder if the dreams are part of a shared consciousness and if they're thread-safe so they could be used from multiple dreams in other people without developing corruption or encountering race conditions. If a dream contained only immutable data, that would prevent corruption from multiple processes manipulating data at the same time. Maybe that's why you can't control dreams, but I have definitely realized I'm in a dream and changed things. Maybe it uses concurrent data structures. (Note to self: read Maurice P. Herlihy & Jeannette M. Wing, "Linearizability: A Correctness Condition for Concurrent Objects," ACM Transactions on Programming Languages and Systems, 1990.)

Someone phones me on my old-school wireless phone, the kind with the antenna that telescopes out six feet like a walkie-talkie, the Gordon Gekko Wall Street phone. They ask me if the bank was open, and I tell them it closed in 1936 or something, based on a ledger book I lifted. Maybe Dillinger robbed it, although I guess he died a few years before that. Allegedly. After I hang up, I suddenly realize it was a felony for me to give out any banking advice without being FDIC-insured, and I start making plans to flee the country.

Can't remember if this actually happened, or if I'm still in the dream, but I'm watching a TV show in a hotel room. I am still in some disorienting loop of time garbage, don't know where I really am, and don't really care anymore. Maybe the TV show is a made-for-TV movie, but I swear the character in it is me. The TV is an old CRT tube set from an unknown manufacturer, and it makes the video look like an Instagram filter, which is fitting because the movie has this bizarre Vaporwave soundtrack and looks like it was filmed by some hipster doofus with a TikTok account full of this junk.

So me, or the character that's me ends up in a weird City With a Secret. Stepford, Wicker Man, City of Ember, whatever. Maybe M. Night wrote it, or maybe I ate before bed. I keep asking people if time is real or how I can get a reuben that's not just a pastrami sandwich with Miracle Whip on it, and everyone says, "Ask the Statue." Nobody will tell me what statue. Never got that reuben, either.

Two commercial breaks later, I'm in a forest next to the village, and there's the statue. It's the dumb marble Vaporwave album cover statue that is almost mandatory on every Bandcamp-released album these days. It even has the pink and purple lights, although I have no idea how they powered them this far out in the woods, and I don't see like a Honda Generator whirring away.

"Hey, eh, what's your problem? Haven't seen you before." The statue is voiced by Burt Reynolds. I think the movie must have been made after the total failure of Stroker Ace, when every movie he made was box office poison and he was desperate for work.

"Yeah, give me a second. Let this asshole go first." I gestured to a dude who looked like he never left his mom's basement. I guess you were supposed to bring an offering to the statue, and I had nothing except a bunch of Motel 6 bar soap and a few low-end towels I stole.

"Dearest statue, I've brought you my grandma's famous ranch casserole. Seven layers of different ranch dressing in it, and uses vintage Cool Ranch Doritos. Fifty-eight dollars of cheese right in here." He sets it on the altar in front of the statue. No response at all. "Dearest statue, my neighbor Fred is an asshole. I want to build a wall that's ten feet high so I don't have to see his stupid face anymore. What kind of bracing do I need to build it that high and put electric wire on the top?"

"You are a fucking idiot," the statue said. "I don't know where you plan on building that fence, but you look stupid enough that you're either going to put it on a utility company easement or on his property, and I'm sure you weren't pulling permits on any of this shit. Also city code says you can't build a fence higher than 3.5 feet in the front yard or six feet on the side or back walls. And the fence permit and the building permit are two different things, and I'm sure you'll fuck that up. And because you're renting and you're not the owner or a state-licensed contractor, you can't do any of this anyway. Go away. And your grandmother's casserole is a god damned war crime. Tell everyone in your family they need to immediately get on the highest dose of Lipitor they can."

I'm still in this dream, or watching this TV show, and suddenly realize - wasn't this a Twilight Zone? I ask ChatGPT, and sort of. "The Old Man in the Cave" — The Twilight Zone, Season 5, Episode 7 (original air date: November 8, 1963) is pretty much the same plot, but no Burt Reynolds. That original story is set in a post-apocalyptic 1974, a decade after a nuclear war. Some villagers obey a mysterious man in a cave that gave them advice on crop rotation or whatever. There's a subplot with some potentially poisoned food cans and a military group that shows up saying they're from the government. In the end, it turns out the man was a computer, and they destroy it and then eat a bunch of nuclear spam, killing everyone in the village.

A townie with a god complex hits the statue with a monster truck. Burt Reynolds dies. Burt Reynolds is played by Norm MacDonald, and he dies. There's a Cloudflare outage and ChatGPT dies. I think I die. My writing career died before it was born, and nobody reads anymore. We all die. I wanted this story to be some long allegory about AI or the problems of life or the general emptiness of everything, but I have no energy to explain any of it.

I wake up on the black gravel of Reynisfjara beach in Iceland, a monochromatic world of black rock, gray water extending all the way across the globe to Antarctica, a fine mist in the air from fifty-foot waves crashing against the basalt shoreline. I can't tell if it's day or night, summer or winter. It is stark desolation and complete nothingness and absolutely terrorizing and beautiful. The dream is over and another one has started.

About the Author

I'm a writer, husband, MBA, photographer, commercial drone pilot, and technologist. My first job was cleaning the bathrooms at a Taco Bell in 1987, and expect to finish my career doing the same thing.

This is the first book I've published with Rumored Books. I don't have the time or energy to explain why I started a new publishing company, so just go with it.

I've lived in North Dakota, Michigan, Indiana, Washington, New York, Colorado, and California. I've been in Oakland for almost twenty years. It's not bad.

This is my 19th book. I have been blogging at Rumored.com since 1997.